D1505570

OMEGA CITY

INFINITY BASE

Diana
Peterfreund

BALZER + BRAY

An Imprint of HarperCollins*Publishers*

Balzer + Bray is an imprint of HarperCollins Publishers.

Omega City: Infinity Base
Copyright © 2018 by Diana Peterfreund

Library of Congress Control Number: 2017959247
ISBN 978-0-06-231091-0 (trade bdg.)

Typography by Carla Weise
18 19 20 21 22 CG/LSCH 10 9 8 7 6 5 4 3 2 1

❖

First Edition

For Louisa, who reaches for the stars

CONTENTS

TRUST NO ONE

MY FATHER ALWAYS TAUGHT ME THAT THE TRUTH WAS WORTH FIGHTING for. For him, the price had been enormous—he'd given up his career, lost Mom, hid away in a cabin in the woods. But I still believed him. It was why I'd convinced my brother and my friends to follow the clues Dr. Underberg had left to the lost underground bunker of Omega City, why I'd decoded the radio messages from the numbers station and sought out the secret labs in Eureka Cove.

Now, because I couldn't stop searching for the truth, my father had been reduced to a pair of twin red lights receding into the inky blackness of the tunnel beneath Eureka Cove. The Shepherds had captured him, and there was nothing I could do about it.

I stood at the door to the biostation, torn in two. I wanted to run after him, but there was no way I could catch up to a truck on foot. Even if I could, did I think I could take on the Shepherds single-handedly?

And it would be single-handedly. Behind me, inside the glowing white bubble of the biostation, my brother and my friends were freaking out, and my mother lay sleeping, half-frozen, on a table. I was pretty sure there was nothing I could do about that, either.

"Gillian!" Savannah shouted, her voice echoing around the bubble-like interior of the station. "Gillian, come back!"

I cast one last look out the door. The lights were gone. Dad was gone.

"Gillian! We need you!"

I swallowed and ran back to my friends. My brother, Eric, was still bent over my mom's unconscious form, squeezing her shoulder and shouting at her to wake up. My best friend, Savannah, was standing nearby, wringing her hands.

The monitor over the table beeped incessantly to indicate that the cooling system the Shepherds had put my mother into had been disrupted. I'd seen how it worked with the chimpanzee we'd revived a few hours ago. All we needed to do was disconnect Mom from this machine, get her away from the cooling pads, and she'd wake up.

Eventually.

Eric was already yanking the pads out from around Mom's body. Thankfully, either he or Savannah had thought ahead far enough to retrieve her clothes from the floor and make sure she stayed covered up. I looked at the pile of clothes remaining on the ground. There were Dad's pants. There were Nate's flip-flops.

And next to them, his hands wrapped tight around Nate's General Tso's Pizza T-shirt, sat Howard. His knees were drawn up to his chest, and he was staring blankly at the floor. I kind of wished I could join him. The Shepherds had his brother, as well as my father. Add that to the list of things I'd screwed up.

"Howard!" I rushed to his side. "It's okay. We'll find them." I touched his shoulder and his elbow shot out, knocking me back on my butt.

"Howard, listen . . . ," I tried again, and again he flailed, this time elbowing me in the chest. Hard.

"Ow!" I rubbed my sore sternum and glared at Howard. Maybe give him a minute. I stood up, then joined my brother, who was shoving Mom's floppy arms into the sleeves of her blouse.

"She's not waking up," Eric said. "She's not waking up."

"It's okay. It takes awhile, remember? It'll be okay." Already, the word "okay" was starting to sound weird in my mouth. I kept saying it, but I no longer knew what it meant. Ohhhhkaaaaay. OK? Why did we say that, anyway? I'm sure Howard would know, if he were in the mood to talk, but at this moment, it seemed bizarre. What a weird combo of letters to mean things were all right.

Because they weren't all right. At all.

Two days ago, we'd come to the Eureka Cove campus of Guidant Technologies to help my father give a speech about Omega City to the engineers here. But after intercepting a code from a secret radio station, my friends and I had started to suspect that Eureka Cove was harboring the Shepherds, a secret society that had buried Omega City and tried to ruin my dad's career.

We'd tracked the origin of the code to this island in the middle of the cove, an island teeming with animal experiments, from hives of dead, genetically engineered bees to tanks of flesh-eating beetles.

We'd also found the Shepherds, because it turned out Guidant was run by Shepherds, and they'd lured us here for far more than a speech.

And now they'd captured my father, and Nate, and if we didn't wake Mom up soon, they'd get the rest of us, too. The beeping of the monitor changed tone, indicating that the process had completed. Savannah ran over with some heavy pads. They were warm to the touch. "Try this," she said. "Maybe they'll help her warm up faster."

"Mom, wake up," Eric said. "Wake up, wake up, wake up."

"Don't waste your time," said a voice. The three of us whirled around.

Dani Alcestis stood at the door, her Omega City utility suit balled up under her arm. She was still in her street clothes, her hair slicked back into a bun at the nape of her neck. "It's not the hypothermic torpor keeping her unconscious. She was tranquilized before they lowered her body temperature. It'll take several hours for the drugs to work their way through her system."

"I thought you'd left with Ms. Mero," I said, narrowing my eyes. I didn't care if Dani did claim to be Dr. Underberg's daughter, or that she was trying to help us. If she were really helping, would we be stuck here right now?

"Change of plan," she replied, and strode forward. "I told you this wasn't going to be easy."

"Where's my father?" I asked her. "Where's Nate?"

She sighed. "They're in hypothermic torpor transport pods." She nodded to the table. "Like your mom is supposed to be. Like *you* are supposed to be."

"Transport . . ." I took a deep breath. "Transporting us *where*?"

"I'll get to that. We've got bigger problems at the

moment." She pointed at Howard, who was still rocking. He hadn't even looked up when Dani came in. "What's with him?"

"What's with him?" Savannah echoed in disbelief. "I don't know, lady. You kidnapped his brother and put him in a hypothermic whatsit. He's a little upset."

Dani rubbed her temples. "I really can't handle temper tantrums right now. You guys need to deal with him, or none of you are going to make it out of here alive."

"What's that supposed to mean?" Eric said. "And what do you expect us to do? This isn't a temper tantrum. This is Howard. He gets like this. And you—you froze the only person who knows how to 'deal with him.'"

Under normal circumstances, this would be where Howard pointed out that nobody froze Nate—that they'd put him in a state of hypothermic torpor. And that Dani had been eating astronaut ice cream with us when it happened. But Howard clearly wasn't listening.

And Dani didn't care. She was the only one who seemed to have the slightest idea what was going on, and certainly the only one who might help us. So fighting with her wasn't really an option. We were alone in a big tent in an underground tunnel and she was our only way out.

I turned to face her. Her expression seemed stern, but as she glanced at each of us in turn, I realized something. Dani had to be at least twenty years older than I was, but for a second all I could see was that she was just as scared as the rest of us. And she should be. We all knew what the Shepherds were capable of. They'd flooded our house and ruined my father's career just because he was poking around the edges of their secrets. They'd forced Dr. Underberg to go into hiding for decades. And Dani probably knew plenty more things, because she *was* a Shepherd.

Or she used to be, anyway. It was all so confusing.

"Okay," I said again, though it still sounded wrong. "Have it your way. We're kids and we're having a temper tantrum. But we do want to get out of here. All of us, and my mom. And we need to get Dad and Nate back, too. So what do we need to do?"

She looked at me. "You need to listen to me, and do exactly as I say."

"We have been," said Eric. "And look where we are!"

"Yeah." Savannah nodded. "How are those plans of yours going?"

I turned to them. "Stop! It's not Dani's fault. She tried to keep us from going to the island, remember? When Dad asked Elana about the numbers station, it was Dani who fed them the lie about it being a Eureka Cove student project. She told Howard and me to run when we were up at the radio tower. If we're here now, it's because . . ." I stopped and tucked my chin into my chest. "It's because of me."

I was the one who insisted on going to the island. I was

the one who kept everyone up all night trying to crack the codes. I was the one who went into Dad's voice mail back home and learned about the invitation to Eureka Cove to start with. Dad never would have known about the trip in time. We were only here because I insisted on going. One last hurrah before Mom moved Eric and me to Idaho.

This was all because of me.

"The first thing you need to do," Dani said, "is stop shouting. You're in a big, empty space in a big, empty tunnel. Your voices carry. I could hear you all the way outside. And if people hear you, they will know that you are not, in fact, isolated and unconscious in your hypothermic transport pods, which is where I told Elana I was putting you."

Eric, Savannah, and I exchanged nervous glances. Howard still didn't look up.

"And what's the second thing we need to do?" Savannah asked quietly.

Dani took a deep breath. "You need to get in the hypothermic transport pods."

"No," said Eric. "No way." He looked back at Mom, still lying on the table, her clothes wrapped around her in a tangle.

"Absolutely not," Savannah added.

Dani shrugged. "Fine. So much for doing exactly as I say . . ."

"How is that supposed to help us?" Eric threw his

hands up in the air. "It doesn't. It puts us exactly where they want us."

"It's the only way I can protect you—"

"I'm not getting frozen," Savannah said. She crossed her arms over her chest. "You can forget it."

I said nothing. I had nothing to say. We were trapped. Dad and Nate were captured, Mom and Howard were out of commission. We'd run out of options. We'd run out of time. All we had was Dani, and she said this was our only move.

Eric turned to me. "You can't be considering this, Gills. Come on. You don't trust her, do you?" He gestured at Dani. "She's one of *Them*, remember? One of the Them-miest Thems there are?"

"Yeah," I said. "And that's probably why she knows exactly how much danger we're in."

"We've been in danger before," he said. "What about with Fiona?"

When we'd been underground in Omega City, Eric had gone through the air vents to reach the others, and left me alone in the communications room. There, Fiona, the ex-Shepherd, had threatened all our lives. She'd told us that if we didn't surrender, she'd seal us all in Omega City forever. We'd ignored her and fought our way out.

But that was different. That was Fiona and two guys who were as lost in Omega City as we were. That was Nate,

Howard, Savannah, Eric, and me with maps and plans and energy to run. This was the Shepherds' home turf. We were far outnumbered. And worst of all, I couldn't even imagine what escape looked like. We didn't just need to get aboveground, we needed to get away from Eureka Cove. And that still wouldn't help Nate and Dad.

"If we get in the pods—" I began to say to Dani.

"Gillian!" Savannah cried.

"Shh!" hissed Dani.

"*If* we get in the pods," I tried again, "then what? How will that help us?"

"I'm not getting frozen," Savannah repeated.

"I won't freeze you," said Dani.

"I'm not getting"—she waved her hands at the machines—"hypothermic torpedoed or whatever, either."

"That's not what I mean," Dani said. "I'm not going to put you guys in torpor. It's a pretty complicated process, and it's not necessary. I do think, however, that I might have to give you a tranquilizer."

"Put us to sleep?" Eric asked, incredulous. "How is that better?"

"I have to get you in the pods, and I need you to stay still and quiet, no matter what happens. I can't have you freaking out in the middle of things." She cast a quick glance at Howard. "But I promise you, this is the only way."

"No," said Eric. "You could stick us in the back of a

truck and cover us with a blanket. You could sneak us out. We could . . . create a diversion . . ."

"Elana wants you in the pods. I told her I'd put you in the pods. I'm already close to blowing my cover. If I don't put you in the pods, and she wants to double-check—and believe me, you don't get to be the leader of the Shepherds and the head of a multibillion-dollar tech company without making sure that the people who work for you are obeying your orders—then we're all doomed. Do you honestly think you could stay still and quiet if you were just pretending to be unconscious? No matter what they do to you?"

I didn't have to answer that. I already knew I couldn't. Maybe Dani was right.

Savannah shuddered, and I saw tears forming in her big, bright eyes. "But we'll be trapped."

Good point. I spoke up. "If something happens to you anyway, if you mess up again, we won't be able to help ourselves."

"I know," Dani said. "And I agree, it's scary. But what the Shepherds are planning to do to you is even scarier."

Savannah whimpered. I put my arms around her and glared at Dani.

Dani grimaced. "I probably shouldn't have said that, huh?"

"Put it on the list of things you shouldn't have done," Eric replied. "Starting with joining the Shepherds."

"And ending somewhere before I threw away my entire life to save you and your family?" she shot back.

Eric's mouth clapped shut.

"Um, can you excuse us for a minute?" I said.

Dani stamped her foot. "We don't have time for this. If someone comes in here and catches me with you—"

"Just a minute!"

"Fine." She turned and strode for the door. "I'm getting the pods."

As soon as she was gone, the three of us huddled up.

"What about Howard?" Savannah asked.

I shook my head. It was like he'd shut down. But no, that wasn't it. He wasn't a robot. But he wasn't paying attention, either. If Nate were here, maybe we could figure out how to talk to him, but meanwhile, we were running out of time.

"We can't wait for him to snap out of it. We have to take a vote." I raised my hand. "Who votes to follow Dani's lead?"

"I can't believe you, Gills," Eric said. "Why? Because she's an Underberg? We're just going to voluntarily let her put us to sleep and take us somewhere?"

"What's the alternative?" I asked.

"Run?" he suggested. "Now, when her back is turned?"

"And what about Mom?" I asked. He looked down. "And Dad?"

"Yeah," said Savannah. "What about your dad? And Nate? We have no idea what the Shepherds plan to do to them."

"And we have no way of finding out from here. We can't run with Mom passed out and Howard . . . doing whatever Howard's doing."

Eric thought about this. "So basically our choice is surrender to Dani now, or get caught by the Shepherds later."

Savannah blinked away a fresh set of tears.

There was a third option, I realized, though it was one I wasn't happy to share with the group. If we refused Dani's offer, she might be forced to capture us herself and turn us over to the Shepherds, for her own protection.

"I don't trust her," I said, "but I can't think of any other way. Not a way that helps Mom or Howard, or Dad, or Nate. I'm sorry, Sav."

"Why?" she said. "I love them, too. And you're right. I can't think of a way to escape this place, either."

Dani returned, wheeling a car loaded with four long gray boxes like coffins—the pods.

I turned to her and squared my shoulders. "Okay." This time I sounded like I meant it. "We'll do what you say."

She beckoned to me. I came close, and she pulled a small syringe dart out of her pocket.

"Wait, needles?" I said, shying back.

"What did you think it was going to be?" She ripped open a foil packet and pulled out an alcohol swab.

"I don't know," I said as she tugged at the neck of my utility suit and wiped down a patch of skin. "A pill or something."

"Takes too long," she said. "This will have you asleep in a minute." I felt a prick where my shoulder met my neck, and a harsh burning sensation shot through the area and spread out across my chest.

"Ow!" I clapped my hand over the spot, then swayed on my feet.

Dani caught me and boosted me into the first of the pods. I lay back against soft, grayish-black padding on the inside.

"She's going to be able to breathe in there, right?" Eric said, hovering over me.

"Yes. The top is full of vents. See?" I looked, but I didn't see anything. She was attaching seat-belt-like straps over my shoulders and across my thighs.

"Iz allride," I slurred at Eric. I tried to make the "OK" sign like in scuba diving but my fingers slipped. Dani pushed my hand into the pod, then flipped a switch near my head.

Was it me falling asleep, or was the padding around me suddenly getting . . . thicker? Softer? I could feel it inflating around the form of my body to hold me into place. I tried to turn my head and couldn't.

Above me, the outline of Dani was growing fuzzy. Her voice floated down to me as if from a great distance. "You know, you were wrong about what you said before."

"Whaaa?" I asked. I think.

"If you'd done what I said yesterday," she whispered, "they'd have you all by now, just as they planned. Our chances were never very good, Gillian, but at least this way, there's still some hope."

I didn't have the energy to respond. Could barely even nod. And the last words I heard were:

"You're the reason you're all still alive."

BACKUP

I OPENED MY EYES TO DIMNESS. NOT COMPLETE BLACKNESS, LIKE THE inside of the padded pod, but the gray-blue darkness of night. I was still in my utility suit, lying on a nicely made bed in what seemed to be a perfectly normal bedroom. I could see the outlines of furniture, pictures on the walls, heavy curtains drawn tight shut over windows . . . and two figures huddled on the floor near the door, their utility suits glinting even in the gloom.

"She's up." I heard a whisper, and one of the suited people turned to me. "Gillian, get down here." It was Savannah.

I sat up, then felt a wave of dizziness wash over me. I

put my hand to my head. "Owww . . ."

"Shh." I think that was Eric. He beckoned to me and I slumped to the floor, then crawled over. "What's going on?" My head was pounding. And how were they up before me? Didn't they get tranquilized, too? "Where are we?"

"Dani's house. Listen." Savannah pressed her ear against the door.

". . . Will not, under any circumstances, do anything to further threaten my children's safety."

Mom! She was awake! And she did not sound happy.

"Now give me back my phone."

"Dr. Seagret, I respect your position. Please try to understand mine. I'm risking my life to have you here. Believe me when I say that calling the police is not going to get you a result that will help your ex-husband or Nate."

"You sound just like him," Mom replied. "Sam."

"Well, then. Ask yourself: Was he right?"

Mom didn't say anything for a long moment. We all crouched there on the floor, listening.

I realized I needed to go to the bathroom. And get a drink of water. And possibly throw up. "Um, guys?" I wavered a little bit on my heels. "I don't . . ." Oh, no, there it was. The bile rose in my throat and I gagged.

"She's puking," said Eric, hopping back. "Yuck, get the garbage can. Quick!" Savannah reached for something in the darkness, but she wasn't quick enough, and I fell on my hands and knees, retching on the carpet.

A moment later, the door burst open, bathing the triangle of carpet where we sat in harsh yellow light. I could see my mother silhouetted on the threshold with Dani right behind her.

"Gillian, sweetie." Mom knelt beside me and put her arm around my shoulders. I was too sick to protest and just leaned in to her, coughing a little. She handed me a tissue, which was when I realized that she was dressed in an Omega City utility suit, too. My *mother*. I was so confused. And my head hurt.

"It's the tranquilizer," Dani said.

"You think?" Mom snapped at her.

"I'll get her some water." Dani looked at the floor. "And some . . . carpet cleaner."

Mom stroked my hair. "Poor baby," she murmured, and for a second, I did feel small again, lying on her lap while she cuddled me. I couldn't remember the last time we'd sat that way. Since she'd come back to town, I wouldn't let her near me. Was it back in the woods, when Dad had made us all live off grid to protect us from Them? No . . . then she was always comforting Eric, who freaked out every time he found bugs in the tent or spiders in his boots. . . .

Another surge of nausea rocked my body. This time I made it to the trash can.

"Shhh," said Mom, rubbing my back. "I'm so sorry

she did this to you, honey. That was not okay."

Well, at least we agreed on one thing. But there was a whole list of not-okay we had to go over.

Dani returned with a glass of water and a wad of wet paper towels. "I've decided I don't really care about the carpet," she said. "Since I'm moving out, anyway."

"Just sip," said Mom to me. She held the glass for me, and I took an obedient sip. "I felt sick when I woke up, too. It'll pass in a few minutes."

"Where is Howard?" I asked, my voice raspy.

"Still out," said Eric.

"I have him in the other room," Dani explained. "He was so upset, I gave him a bigger dose than the rest of you."

"You did *what*?"

She shrugged a single shoulder. "He fought me."

I sat up in a panic. And we'd all been out cold and couldn't help him! "You had no right to—"

"Exactly," interrupted Mom. "Just as I've been telling her." She squeezed my shoulder. "Honey, just sit here for a few minutes. You don't want to be sick again."

There were a lot of things I didn't want, and though vomiting was pretty high up there on the list, making sure Howard hadn't been hurt was well above it. I pushed myself off Mom and ignored the sour, roiling feeling in my tummy.

"I feel fine." I gingerly stood and started out the door

with Mom right on my heels.

The bedroom door led out to an eat-in kitchen. I shuffled out, blinking slowly as I got my bearings. Dani's house resembled all the other Guidant model homes, though much more lived-in than the one they'd given us during our visit. It still had all the sleek, computerized appliances and the corporate beige color scheme, but the furniture looked like it came from my grandparents' old house, and there were goofy magnets on the fridge and strange, geometric shapes cluttering up the window ledges and the corkboard over the kitchen counter.

Beyond the kitchen I could see a pair of wide glass double doors leading into what might have been a living room, or an office, or both. Floor-to-ceiling bookshelves were crammed with thick textbooks, periodicals, and binders marked with neatly stenciled labels like "Test Flights 1983–1989" and "Launch Manual 3118." There was a sofa, a few old-fashioned-looking chairs, some antique end tables and lamps, and a bunch of framed photographs on all the walls and side tables.

I peered closer at the pictures. Most appeared to be Dani as a child or a teenager. In many, she was posing with an older, dark-skinned woman that was most likely her mother. There were pictures of them in front of Christmas trees and building sand castles on a beach, at fancy parties and in front of the Eiffel Tower. In one black-and-white portrait, Dani's mother—very young—stood in cap and gown with a diploma. In a grainy color photo, she wore an impressive bouffant hairdo and posed in front of some NASA ship I'm sure Howard would be able to recognize on sight.

None of the pictures showed Dr. Underberg.

"Where's Howard?" I asked.

"In my bedroom," said Dani, pointing. "Sleeping."

I still needed to see. I pushed the door open and headed inside. The room was dim, with tiny slivers of amber light from the streetlamp outside sifting through the edges of the tightly drawn curtains and reflecting off the silver surface of Howard's utility suit. He was laid out on his back on the bed, and he was, as Dani had promised, fast asleep.

"Howard?" I asked.

"You should leave him alone until he wakes up," said Dani from the threshold.

I should have left him alone long before this. Before his brother got kidnapped and he got tranquilized and we all got trapped here in Dani's weird retro town house.

Howard began to stir. His eyelids fluttered open and he focused on me. I braced myself, expecting more rage.

"Where's Nate?" he whispered.

My heart sank. This was worse than Howard being angry at me. "I don't know yet."

Howard nodded miserably and his eyes drifted shut.

Mom's hands landed on my shoulders and she steered me out of the room and toward the kitchen table. "Let's get some food in you," she said gently. "It'll settle your stomach."

I sincerely doubted that, but I let her guide me into a chair. The others were circling the table as well. "I'm not hungry."

"Really?" said Mom. "The way I heard it, all you've eaten in twenty-four hours is some freeze-dried ice cream. Now sit. I have no idea what you kids have been up to, but a grown-up is here now, and you're going to listen." I glanced up to see her staring pointedly at Dani as if she, too, were a kid in need of parental guidance.

"Yes, Mom," said Eric, and flopped into a chair.

"Yes, Mrs. Dr. S," said Sav, following suit.

Dani placed a pot of chicken soup, a sleeve of saltine crackers, and a bunch of bowls and spoons on the table, and began ladling out servings. I took a sniff. Canned.

Just like Dad used to make after he burned dinner.

This time the lump in my throat wasn't vomit.

"Now," said Mom, standing at the end of the table. "You kids will have to excuse me and Dani, but we were in the middle of a private conversation, and I want to finish it while you're eating—"

"No, you weren't," mumbled Eric.

"Excuse me?" she asked.

"No, you weren't in a private conversation, Mom. We heard everything." He slumped in his seat, his shoulders hunched. "I don't know what you think you're protecting us from, either. Is there anything bad going on that we don't know about? You'd still be a Popsicle if it wasn't for us. We're all in the same boat. Dad and Nate have been kidnapped, this place is crawling with Shepherds, and we can't even call the cops."

Mom stared at him. I stared at him, too. Who would have thought mama's boy Eric over there would disagree with any of her ideas?

"Eric's right," I said. "If you leave us out of the loop, we're just going to get even more frightened than we already are."

"More like you'll just come up with your own scheme," Mom replied, eyeing me shrewdly. "You think I don't know how you guys operate? Fine. We'll talk here. On one condition."

"What?"

"This is *not* a democracy. There will be no voting. I am your mother, and you will do as I say." She looked at Savannah. "You, too."

We three looked at one another.

I thought about what Dani had said to me right before I'd passed out—that if we hadn't kept pushing and searching and fighting, we might all be dead right now. I thought about those lonely hypothermic transport pods, and wondered what had happened to Dad and Nate. They weren't dead, right? Just . . . in stasis, like Mom and that chimp.

"But . . . ," I began in a small voice, "you *do* want to save Dad, right?"

"Oh, honey!" cried Mom. "Of course I do!"

Some tiny knot inside me relaxed at her words.

"And Nate, of course. But I want to do it without putting anyone else in danger. This isn't a game. These people—these Shepherds—have proved they're dangerous. I know that better than anyone."

"What happened when they caught you?" Savannah asked.

Mom bit her lip for a second. "We were in the self-driving car. The one that was supposed to take us back to our van. And it just . . . stopped. It wouldn't go; it wouldn't answer any of our commands. And then the doors wouldn't unlock. We tried calling someone, but neither of us could get a signal on our cell phones. Can you believe it? At Guidant, where you think reception would be amazing. That's what made me worry."

"Worry what?" Savannah asked.

Mom looked sheepish. "Worry that it was something more than the car just being broken. I was married to Sam Seagret for over a decade. Some things rub off."

"What did you do?"

"Nate was totally calm, I have to hand it to him. I could see the guy Sam had written about, helping you kids when you were stuck in Omega City." Mom smiled at the memory. "He kicked the window out of the car, then climbed out. It was pretty cool. He was helping me when some people came out of nowhere. They shot him with something, and he went right down."

More tranquilizers. I saw how quickly it had dropped the chimpanzee. I wondered if there was a bigger dose in those darts than I'd gotten from Dani.

"I screamed—for a second I thought they'd shot him with, you know, a gun or something. So I went into my purse and I pepper-sprayed them."

"Wow!" cried Savannah. "Good going, Mrs. Dr. S!"

I goggled at my mother with newfound appreciation. I didn't even know she carried pepper spray in her purse. She certainly hadn't before she'd moved out. Elana had mentioned that my mother had put up a fight. I wondered how many Shepherds she'd taken down.

"Well, it didn't work. More guys came at me and that's pretty much the last thing I remember."

I hugged myself and tucked my chin into my chest. They'd never even gotten off the Guidant campus. While we'd been tubing, and having dinner with Elana and Anton and Dani—while we'd been cracking codes and exploring the Shepherds' secret island base—all that time, they'd been captured. Was that the Shepherds' plan for us? Kidnap us the moment we tried to leave? Or did they always intend to capture us? Had we narrowly missed them yesterday morning when we gave our car the wrong address, then sneaked off in a pair of kayaks for the unmarked island in the middle of Eureka Cove?

"Until I woke up here, in this ridiculous outfit, with four kids passed out all around me," Mom finished. "And now Dani says she's not working for the Shepherds anymore, and wants to help us escape and find your father and Nate, and honestly, that's about as far as we've gotten."

I frowned into my soup. That wasn't very far. Did Dani even know where my father was?

"Now, from what Dani has told me, the reason we were all brought here was to be held as hostages, correct?"

"Sort of," said Dani. "Elana wanted to recruit Dr. Seagret—the other Dr. Seagret—into the Shepherds.

"Your father is one of Dr. Underberg's biggest fans. His biggest cheerleader. You children are the only people who have seen him in decades, and it immediately became clear to us that he holds you in high regard, too."

"Because he was willing to take us into outer space with him?" Eric asked. "I just thought that was because he was crazy."

Dani went on. "He deeply, deeply cares about the few people in the world he loves. Elana believed that by getting you on her team, she'd sufficiently discourage Dr. Underberg from trying to wreck her plans."

"Why did she think that?" Eric asked.

"Because it's worked before," Dani said softly.

Oh. It worked with her. Dani and her mom. When Dr. Underberg had quarreled with the Shepherds and fled, he'd left Dani's mother behind alone and pregnant. She'd remained a Shepherd and raised her daughter in the organization. And Dr. Underberg had disappeared.

"Have you spoken to your father recently, Dani?" Mom asked.

"Dr. Underberg," Dani corrected. "It's not like I . . . know him or anything. It's been three days since I've gotten a message. But that's not unusual. He goes dark often, especially when he's worried that the Shepherds have located him."

"I'm pretty familiar with men like that," Mom said drily.

"But he must know we didn't get recruited, right?" I asked. "You told him, right?" Maybe that's why he'd gone dark. He thought everyone had turned against him again.

"It never came to that." Dani shrugged. "Elana saw that your father wasn't going to fall in line, and neither were any of you. And if you can't join them, beat them."

"I think it's the other way around—" Eric started to say. "Oh. Beat *us*."

"Right," said Mom. "We were supposed to be hostages."

Dani shook her head. "Hostages implies that if Dr. Underberg does what Elana wants, she'll let your dad and Nate go."

"She's not going to let them go?" I asked. Mom already looked like she regretted letting us kids listen in on this.

Dani met my eyes. "No. She's going to use them as bait."

I was going to be sick again.

3

LAUNCH PLANS

BAIT? TAKE IT FROM A GIRL WHO SPENT THE LAST TWO YEARS WITH A creek off her back porch—you never, ever wanted to be referred to as "bait."

My immediate thought was that we had to rescue them, but then again, wasn't that how bait worked? To lure in the things you hadn't caught yet? Things like us?

Eric toyed with his spoon. Savannah nibbled a cracker. Both looked at me.

And I had no idea what to say.

Just then, Dani's phone buzzed on the table. I nearly jumped out of my seat. Dani put her fingers to her lips and pressed a button.

"Yes, Elana?"

Elana's voice drifted out, tiny and tinny, but still packing quite the punch. "I see you're back home—"

My mouth opened in a silent gasp. How did she know?

"Yes," Dani said, amazingly calm. "It was a very long day. I thought I'd get a few hours of sleep—"

"Did you manage to complete their voice modeling settings? You also went to the guesthouse."

This time I shivered. Did she know everywhere Dani had gone?

"Yes, I took the recordings and the personal effects."

I met Savannah's eyes across the table. *We were recorded?* she mouthed at me. I just shrugged. Guidant apparently tracked everything. Being recorded seemed like small potatoes in a world where some of us had also been kidnapped and frozen.

"Do you need the voice models?" Dani asked

"Not at present, but we'll have to have a story prepared."

"Of course," Dani replied, giving Savannah a careful glance. "By the time I'm done, Savannah Fairchild's mother won't know the difference."

Savannah stiffened in her seat at the sound of her name.

Dani cleared her throat. "Where is the cargo at present?"

The *cargo*. She meant the pods. Dad and Nate and . . . us.

"Out at the launch facility," Elana said. "I told Anton I want no delay."

"I understand. I'll have the models ready right away." She clicked the phone off.

Savannah pounced. "What was that all about? Why were you talking about me?"

"Because I want Elana to think the reason I'm hiding away in my house is because I'm training your voice model applications."

"Our what?"

"It's an AI program that can mimic your presence on voice calls," Dani said, as if she were still our official Eureka Cove tour guide.

"Wait," I cried. "You're training an *artificial intelligence* program to use our voices?"

"It's not as interesting as it sounds. Just a standard conversation bot with an overlay using your individual voices to create a vocabulary gleaned from actual recordings of words as well as random syllable combination and personality inflections."

"Right," Mom said slowly. "*Standard.*"

I had no idea what Dani meant, either.

Dani didn't seem to hear my mother's sarcasm. "Just in case anyone calls and wants to talk to you. We did it with your father yesterday."

I thought back to the phone conversation I'd had with

my father on the island cliff, and how baffled I'd been at his sudden one-eighty on everything he'd taught me. He'd said, *This isn't about freedom. This is about being safe.*

I'd been so scared I'd tossed the phone off the cliff.

But now the truth burst from my lips. "I never spoke to my father yesterday at all!"

"Probably not," Dani admitted. "I completed your father's voice model the day he arrived here."

She sounded so calm. My fists clenched on the table. "Why did you do that?" I said, seething.

Dani looked confused. "It's my job? Or was my job."

"It still is," Eric pointed out. "You just promised Elana you'd make voice bots of us."

"Eric," Mom said, putting her hand on his shoulder. "This isn't a good thing."

He shook it off and narrowed his eyes at Dani. "I know it isn't good. If she can fake our voices, she can fake us saying anything she wants. She can have a fake Savannah call up her mother and say she's running away from home and that will explain why none of us are ever heard from again."

Savannah let out an indignant cry.

"Well, I'd probably not do that," Dani said, still sounding bizarrely matter-of-fact. "That would trigger a manhunt. I'd just program the bot to have Savannah and Dr. Seagret, for instance, explain to her mother that they were extending your trip by a few days, until we could figure out a reasonable explanation for your disappearance. . . ." She trailed off. "You know what? Any way I describe this to you probably sounds terrible."

"Yes," Mom said flatly. "Because it *is* terrible."

Dani looked a little sheepish, which was ironic, given that she was a Shepherd.

"This is also a good cover story," she said. "For any sounds coming from this house that might get picked up from recording devices in my neighbors' houses or out on the street."

"How much of this place is bugged?" Mom asked, astonished.

"All of it," I grumbled. We'd checked ourselves into Shepherd central. Dr. Underberg had to hide away underground to get away from them. Dad had to take us all into the woods for a month. And now we thought we could hide out in their headquarters?

I looked around Dani's house again, at the books and the photos and the out-of-place furniture. There was nothing of Underberg's here. We were entirely at Dani's mercy, and I wasn't entirely sure we could trust her. Even if she was telling the truth about who she was, she was also a Shepherd.

Mom dropped into a seat and rubbed her temples in frustration. "So, what now? We make a run for it?"

"We can't do that until we have Dad and Nate!" I

turned to Dani. "Where's the launch facility? Can we go there and get them?"

"*What* is the launch facility, you mean," Eric corrected. "What are they launching?"

Dani looked pained.

"I know what it is," said a voice from behind us. I turned. Howard leaned against the door to the bedroom, looking as pale and weak as I felt. He held some papers in his hands. "Or at least, I have a guess."

He held out a pile of photocopied sheets. The top one showed a diagram with so many shapes and arcs and parts that I could hardly tell what I was looking at.

Neither, apparently, could Savannah. "What is it, Howard?"

"This?" he said. "This is the plan for a space station. Whatever they're launching, I think it's going there."

"HOWARD," MY MOTHER said kindly, as we all stared, "how are you feeling?"

"Give me that." Dani rounded the table, her hand outstretched to snatch the plans back.

"Don't touch me!" Howard yelped. He took off in the opposite direction.

"If you'd just—" Dani took another step, and Howard jumped over the back of the couch and into the living room.

"Stay away from me!" he shouted again, backing up stiffly. He squeezed his eyes shut.

Maybe he had the right idea.

"Stay away from him!" I echoed, and shot out of my chair. As Dani approached, I vaulted over the back of the couch and planted my feet on the seat cushions. "Mom, help us."

Mom stepped in between Dani and the path to the living room. "Dani, you attacked this child. Don't you think you should keep your distance?"

Dani paused, her lips pursed. "I didn't attack him. I—"

"You tranquilized him," Mom said, her voice calm, her hands held up, palm out, like a traffic guard.

"I tranquilized all of you."

"Yeah," I said. "But Howard fought back."

Mom cast a quick, warning glance at me. "Gillian"— I bristled, but then she finished her sentence—"is right. If we're going to keep working together, I need your assurances that you will not hurt or attack these children again."

"I *saved* you," Dani insisted. "And I'm giving up everything to do it. Do you have any idea where you'd be right now if I hadn't risked everything?"

With Dad and Nate, or possibly worse. I remembered again what Dani said just before I'd blacked out. We were lucky to be alive.

"I'm sorry you don't like my methods, but it's not like we have many options."

"That's not good enough," Mom replied. "You want us to put our trust in you, and not call the cops right now, but you haven't proved yourself very trustworthy."

Dani raised her arms in frustration. "You're here, aren't you? Not frozen or dead. Standing in my house? Eating my soup? Two minutes ago, that kid was asleep in my bed."

"And six hours before that you knocked him out against his will." Mom remained firm.

But so did Dani. "Dr. Seagret," she said slowly, "may I speak to you privately?"

"What?" I cried. "No fair. We promised."

Mom shot me another look, and this one was icy. Then she herded Dani into her office and shut the door.

I turned to Howard. "Are you okay?"

He looked down at the papers in his hand. "I don't like her."

"I'm sorry she hurt you." I guess I hadn't realized he really wasn't listening when we all agreed to let Dani knock us out and stick us in the pods.

"Are you sure she's really Dr. Underberg's daughter?"

I pressed my lips together. I was. At least, I was sure that Dani believed it. Nothing else made any sense.

Eric and Savannah joined us in the living room. "So, what is this?"

"I found it in her bedroom," Howard said. "They look like schematics for a space station. Look at the date." He pointed to a block of text near the key on the first page.

Infinity Base—1979. Wow, these were ancient. My eyes scanned the rest of the text, then grew wide.

"Howard! Look at the name!"

Designed by Aloysius Underberg.

He nodded vigorously. "Well, Dr. Underberg did design rocket ships. It stands to reason he'd design a space station, too."

"But the Shepherds didn't *build* a space station," Eric said.

"No one thought they built Omega City, either," I pointed out.

"That's different," said Eric. "Omega City was underground. They were able to hide it. You can't tell me there's been a space station floating up there for forty years and no one has ever seen it. Dad's friends would be all over something like that."

"I don't think it's been there for forty years." Howard flipped to another page. "Look, this update is from 2013."

I looked down at the newer plan. It looked similar to Underberg's original design, but sleeker. The key was marked *Infinity Base (Capella).*

"Capella," said Savannah. "That's the name of the Guidant satellite. What if—what if they used launching the satellite as a cover to launch this into space?"

Eric stared at her. "Don't you turn into a conspiracy theorist now, too."

"I'm not." Savannah's voice was frantic. "Because this is no theory. Look around: we're living it."

"But you can't have something as big as a space station up there and no one notices it," Eric argued. "Thousands of people have telescopes on their back porches. There are astronomers all over the world. Look at all those pictures we saw in the Capella lab back on Eureka Cove. Howard, tell them."

True. On the tour of the Guidant engineering labs the other day, they'd shown us wall-size images of the pictures the Capella telescope was sending back. "Well, they have to be hiding it somehow."

"No way," said Eric.

I whirled on him. "How can you say that, after everything you've seen? What about all that stuff we found on the island? All the tests they were doing on those space chimps? The research we found said they were in orbit, remember? Where do you think they were? Elana said they are launching Dad and Nate. Launching *where*?"

Eric grimaced, and I suddenly realized—it was easier for him to believe there was no Infinity Base. Because if it didn't exist, then Dad wasn't going anywhere.

But before I could say anything else, the door to Dani's

office opened, and she and Mom emerged. Dani's mouth was set in a tight line, and Mom looked subdued and pale, her expression so much like Eric's at this moment that my throat tightened around a sudden sob.

They were terrified. Both of them. I wondered if I looked like that, too.

Eric snatched the papers out of Howard's hands and waved them in the air. "Is this thing real?" he asked Dani accusingly.

"Yes."

"Is it where they're sending my father?"

"Yes."

The papers slipped from his fingers and scattered across the floor. Eric dropped onto the couch cushions.

I blurted, "But they haven't sent them yet, right? We can still stop it?"

Dani hesitated. "I don't know. I mean, maybe we can go out to the launch facility and try to get to their pods before they are loaded onto the shuttle, but—"

"But what?" I exclaimed. "Let's go. Let's do that right now!"

"Gillian, calm down," Mom said. "We can't go running off without a plan."

The plan was we stopped them from shooting Dad into space. Period.

Howard bent to scoop up the Infinity Base papers. "I

can't believe Nate gets to go to space. He wouldn't even let me go."

"*Gets?*" Savannah asked, incredulous. "He's a prisoner! Also, he won't even know. He's frozen."

"Hypothermic torpor," Howard grumbled, as if he didn't think this made much of a difference. As if Nate was somehow lucky he'd been kidnapped and frozen, as long as it meant he got to go to space.

"Why?" Eric asked softly. "Why would they do this?"

"To get to Dr. Underberg," Dani said.

We all looked at her quizzically.

Dani sighed. "Right now, Underberg is basically untouchable in his rocket ship. They can't catch him. They can't stop him."

"Good," I said. At least there was one person on our side the Shepherds couldn't mess with any longer.

"Stop him from what?" Mom asked.

"For the past few months, he's been interfering with the operation of Infinity Base. Gathering information. Threatening to expose the Shepherds and their lies. Until recently, he was waiting between staff trips up there and even boarding himself, usually to steal our resources. In fact, that's how he and I first got in touch."

"You've been in space?" Howard said, seeming to snap out of his reverie. "How many times?"

"Enough," Dani said. "And once as part of an

investigative team to try to figure out some irregularities happening at the station. I figured out who was to blame, and was able to keep the truth hidden from the others for a little while."

"Let me get this straight," said Mom. "Your father is threatening to expose Elana Mero as a Shepherd."

"Yes, and reveal the truth about the Capella satellite."

"What truth?" Mom asked.

Savannah looked down at the papers Howard was gathering. "That there is no Capella satellite," she said, her voice flat.

Dani nodded. "It's a front for launching the space station."

Savannah's eyebrows furrowed. "But then, where are all those pictures coming from?"

"Thank you!" Eric cried from the couch. "And how are you hiding this space station from every telescope in the world?"

"We don't control every telescope, it's true. But where does most image processing occur? On a Guidant computer, using a Guidant program. Guidant has access to vast caches of data. We very carefully monitor what astronomers are passing around. Then we . . . massage the data until we have hidden any images of the base, and get appropriate alternative pictures of our own."

"You're hacking real astronomers and stealing their

stuff?" I asked. "Just to hide the existence of your space station?"

"That's not the only reason." Dani sounded a little contrite. "I'm sure you can figure out the other."

I thought about it for a second, about all the things Elana, Anton, and Dani had said at dinner the other day, about all the things we'd seen on the island, and my breath caught in my throat.

"Because one day you might want to make it seem like an asteroid will strike the planet and kill everyone, like what happened to the dinosaurs." I narrowed my eyes. "So you can cause a panic. So you can manipulate everyone on Earth into believing the world is coming to an end and they have to abandon the planet."

"Well, so the Shepherds have the ability to do so, yes," Dani said. "If the need should arise."

I wanted to plop down on the couch next to Eric. This was big. Way bigger than Omega City and Dr. Underberg. Way bigger than the experiments on Eureka Cove. If the Shepherds could convince people the world was going to end, they could do anything they wanted.

"But . . . Dr. Underberg. He's trying to expose you."

Dani nodded. "It would be a disaster, not just for the Shepherd cause, but for Guidant Technologies. That's why she needed you."

"I don't understand."

"Dr. Underberg knows the only way the Shepherds can get to him is if he dares to go back to Infinity Base, so he's been keeping his distance. But if someone he cares about is there . . ."

"Like Dad," I whispered. "And Nate."

"He's the only one who can save them up there. He'll have to go back for them. And, when he does, Elana will have him right where she wants him."

THE WRONG STUFF

"WE HAVE TO GO GET DAD!" I CRIED.

"We have to go to the police," Mom said at the same time.

"Explain to me what you'd say in that phone call." Dani folded her arms. *"Hello, officer. I think the president and CEO of Guidant Technologies has kidnapped my ex-husband and his neighbor's kid and are sending them to a secret space station. Something like that?"*

Mom frowned. "No, actually. More like how I was attacked by Guidant security, unjustly imprisoned, and how I haven't seen the young man I was taking care of since that time—oh, and also, my ex-husband is missing on the campus, too. They'd have to account for them."

"Would they?" Dani looked annoyed. "I assure you, all the campus security logs say you and your family checked out yesterday and no one has seen you since."

I could believe that. If Guidant was hacking telescopes, they could fake whatever they wanted.

"But you could back us up," Mom argued.

Dani shook her head. "The only card we have left is that no one at Guidant knows I'm working with you. I'd like to keep it that way as long as possible."

"Oh, really?" Mom crossed her arms. "Can't you just tranquilize anyone who gets in your way?"

"No," Dani replied through gritted teeth. "You made me promise not to do that again, *remember?*"

We all looked at Mom. Well, that was a relief. I wondered what else they'd talked about while they were shut away in Dani's office.

"Yes," Mom said, "because apparently in Shepherd world, you are never taught that attacking children and drugging them against their will is generally frowned upon."

"Yes, and we're also taught excellent methods of evading police and government interference to achieve our goals. Trust me, the cops are not going to help you."

"That's just it," Mom replied, her tone toxic, "I *don't* trust you."

I blew out a sigh of frustration. This was getting us nowhere. We needed to go find Dad. Now. Before it was too late.

"Please," I begged. "We have to try to get my father back."

"How?" Savannah asked.

"The same way Dani got us out," I said. "She can drive to the launch facility and bring back their pods. But she has to do it before they get put on a spaceship and launched into orbit."

"That's an excellent idea," Mom said suddenly. "Dani should do that right now. I'll stay with the children."

Dani glared at my mother. "Not on your life. You aren't sneaking out of here without my help. You'd be caught in a second, and then I'd be done for, too."

"I have no idea what you mean," Mom replied lightly.

Dani and my mother continued their staring contest for another few seconds, then Dani turned to me. "Gillian, I'll need your help to get your father."

I knew what Mom wanted, but I couldn't pass on a chance to save Dad. "Okay."

"No!" my mother snapped. I wasn't sure if it was at me or at Dani.

"This is the only option."

"I will not allow you to manipulate my children or put them in danger."

"Come on, Dr. Seagret. You and I both know they're already in danger."

Mom's shoulders slumped, defeated, and as I turned toward Eric, Howard, and Savannah, I saw that Dani's words had landed. Hard. They all looked scared to death.

And I was pretty sure I was right there with them.

"NOW, WHAT'S THE rule?" Dani said for what had to be the hundredth time. She sounded like my mother.

"Stay hidden," I replied. I lay on the floor in the back-seat of Dani's car, covered by a beige blanket.

"And?"

"And don't get involved." I sighed. The whole ride out to the launch facility, she'd made me repeat the promises I'd made to her and Mom before we'd left. Dani said she needed someone to serve as lookout, and help drive the get-away car.

Except it was a self-driving car, so it was really more like *instruct* the getaway car when it was time to get away.

"And pay attention to my texts," she added.

I nodded, clutching Dani's phone in my hand. She'd installed her own voice model on the device, since her car would be keyed to her identity and voice, and would only work on her command. I could type in commands and the phone would speak in Dani's own voice. "Yes. To the cargo door or the truck depot, depending on where you find Dad and Nate."

"And if I tell you to run?"

"Back home to your place to get the others, don't wait for you," I recited dutifully. That was the part of the plan I didn't like. Mom and Dani expected me to just abandon all hope of rescuing Dad and Nate at the first sign of trouble. "But if they catch you, aren't they going to think it's odd that your car is driving around? Won't they wonder who it is in your house?"

"If they catch me," Dani said, "we've got bigger problems."

I was quiet for a moment, considering that. Dani was our only hope right now, the only person on the entire Guidant campus who we could trust.

Or at least *sort of* trust.

"Thank you for doing this," I blurted. "You know . . . giving up your life and your home and stuff. For us."

"It's not for you." There was something odd in her voice, some little catch I'd never heard before, and I wished I could lift up the blanket and look her in the face. She cleared her throat and went on. "I told you. I think they're making a mistake. This whole thing with your father, with Underberg . . . it's just wrong."

"It's not too late to make it right," I suggested. "My dad will know how to do it, how to get the truth about the Shepherds out there."

She snorted. "Right. The truth. Sometimes I forget I'm talking to a child."

I picked up the corner of the blanket and peered up at her. "What's that supposed to mean?"

She turned in her seat and met my eyes. "It means there's no such thing as 'the truth,' Gillian. Just what people decide they want to believe is right and wrong. What they are willing to fight for and what they aren't."

"That's not . . ." I trailed off before I said something she'd laugh at, like *that's not true.*

"Think about it. We're using up the Earth's resources at an alarming rate. We kill off entire species, burn fossil fuels, make the planet warmer. Look at all the problems we're seeing due to climate change—droughts and floods and crazy weather and ice caps melting. It'll be a disaster and the human race will suffer. That's the 'truth,' isn't it?"

"Um . . . I mean, yes?"

"But other people say that story causes enormous trouble for people by taking away their fossil fuel jobs or forcing them to use different farming or manufacturing methods that are more expensive or more difficult or won't feed or employ or support as many people. It would be a disaster.

The human race would suffer. And *that's* the truth, too, isn't it?"

"I don't know." Maybe I should hide back under my blanket.

She leaned in toward me and dropped her voice. "They are *both* the truth. The climate is changing, and it's our fault, and we're hurting the planet and ourselves. But if we stop the practices that are hurting the planet, then we'll hurt people who rely on those practices. All these stories can be true at once. And if they are all equally true, then they are all equally false as well."

A lump rose in my throat, and it took a minute before I could trust myself enough to speak. "There's still right and wrong."

"Sure there is," Dani said. "We all learn right from wrong, don't we? Except we don't all learn the same right and the same wrong. Your father taught you secrets were wrong. The Shepherds taught me they were right, because they served a higher purpose. That's *our* story, our truth. The Earth will not be able to support humanity forever, whether it's something we do to it, or something that happens all by itself, like an astronomical event. And you can't have it both ways. People are either going to hurt now, or hurt later, and you have to make that decision. The Shepherds make the decision to hurt the people now and protect the people later. That's what being a Shepherd means." She sat back in her seat and stared out the windshield. "Except now I'm throwing that all away."

"Because you decided to fight for something else?"

Dani said nothing for a long moment, and then spoke. "You promised to stay hidden, remember?"

We sat in silence for a few more minutes, then the car pulled to a stop.

"You know the drill," she warned me one last time, then departed.

I lay there, hidden, and thought about what Dani had said. I didn't like it. The truth was real, a real thing, that could be touched and held and seen like Omega City or the Underberg battery. It could be researched and revealed, like one of Howard's codes or my father's histories. It was more—had to be more—than just whatever story you decided to believe.

In my hands, the phone buzzed. I checked the screen, expecting to see a text from Dani telling me where to go. But instead I found the display showed a call coming in.

From Elana Mero.

The phone buzzed and buzzed. I didn't know what Elana was used to. Did Dani always answer her calls? Was Dani even now answering her other phone, wherever she happened to be?

The phone stopped vibrating for a moment. Then it gave one long, slightly different buzz.

A text from Elana.

Why are you at the launch facility?

I swallowed thickly. That's right; the Shepherds could track everyone, all the time. I thought I knew the drill, but we hadn't planned for me to actually speak to Elana Mero.

Dani?

Hands shaking, I typed back.

Just checking that everything is ready with the cargo.

Was that something Dani would say? Was it something she would do? Maybe I should just ignore these messages.

Too late for that, isn't it? You're supposed to be getting the voice models ready. Anton has the launch covered. It's out of your hands now.

I had no idea what that meant. Maybe I should text Dani and tell her to get back here and talk to her boss before I ruined everything. I didn't dare respond.

The phone began to vibrate with a call again. Elana! I wasn't sure what to do this time. I could hardly pretend

Dani didn't have her phone on her. We'd just been texting! The vibrations went on and on.

One missed call. Two. Elana was not taking no for answer. What if she sent someone over to Dani's house? I was putting everyone in danger.

The phone buzzed again. My hand started to shake as I thought about Eric and Mom and my friends. They were sitting ducks at Dani's house.

Wait! I could use the voice model program. Except that was probably way against Mom and Dani's rules. I whimpered. Any second the phone would go to voice mail. Again.

Before I could talk myself out of it, I held my breath, switched to the right program, and pressed the answer button.

"Hello," I typed, and Dani's voice spilled from the speaker.

"I know you're upset," Elana said without preamble. "But you have to understand this is for the best."

My lips closed over a squeak of protest and my fingers moved furiously over the keys. "No, I don't understand." Dani's voice spoke all my words. "The Seagrets are innocent. You should let them go."

"Right," said Elana. "With all the information they have and nothing to hold over them? Do you know how much damage they can do to this organization? Alone was bad enough, but with Underberg threatening all our work? We have to protect Guidant, even if that means sacrificing Infinity Base."

My eyes narrowed. She was doing this to protect Guidant? Her stupid tech company? I thought Shepherds sacrificed everything for the good of humanity.

"What about the Shepherds?" I typed and Dani asked.

Elana gave a world-weary sigh. "You and Anton, I swear. I feel like I spend half my life cleaning up his messes. Stop being such purists. Those old ideals are nonsense. No one in the last generation had the slightest ability to imagine what we could become. They thought we had to work with governments to achieve our goals. Aloysius Underberg, your mother, playing nice all those years with NASA . . . it was a waste of time. We have more power, more resources. Protect Guidant and we can make a hundred Infinity Bases. Destroy Guidant, and the entire Shepherd mission will go down in flames."

I remained quiet.

"Come on, Dani, I know you agree. The Shepherds are what matters. We protect our own, but you know that means making compromises. You're used to that."

Except Dani had turned on the Shepherds . . . hadn't she?

I felt a low rumbling all around me. "What is that?" I typed furiously, though Dani's voice sounded oddly calm.

"The launch, of course. I'm not wasting any more time. It should rendezvous with Infinity Base in about twenty-four hours."

I opened my mouth to scream and the door of the car flung open. Dani plucked the phone out of my hands and hung up.

I lay on the floor of the car, gasping for breath.

They'd shot my father into space.

They'd shot my father into space.

"Breathe," Dani said, hopping into the front seat and closing the door behind her. "We've got a lot of work to do."

SIX SIDES TO EVERY STORY

"THE GOOD NEWS," DANI ANNOUNCED, IN HER AGGRAVATINGLY MATTER-of-fact way, "is that I did hack into the digital output and life-support system of your transport pods to make it seem like you were all safely stowed away in stasis. They think you're part of the payload on the transport shuttle. No one will be looking for you for at least twenty-four hours."

"Oh, goody," said Eric.

Meanwhile, my father was shooting into space, a prisoner of the Shepherds, who wanted him and Dr. Underberg dead.

By this time, we'd all convened in Dani's living room. I was still feeling a little weak and was curled up on the couch, idly flipping through photo albums of Dani and other Shepherds posing in front of early rocket launch tests. It was all I was capable of. I'd hyperventilated the whole way back to Dani's house, then thrown up again, for good measure.

If it was so hard for us to get to Dad when he was merely in hypothermic torpor in the back of a Shepherd truck, how would we ever save him . . . up there?

Mom was presiding over us from the big armchair, and Eric sat at her feet, knees drawn up to his chest. Nearby, Howard knelt in front of Savannah, the top half of his utility suit bunched around his waist, while she tried to reattach the zipper pull he'd broken off yesterday.

No one seemed to know what came next.

"So what now?" I asked. "What do we do now?"

Dani looked at Mom. Mom looked at Dani. Neither said anything, but they didn't need to. They thought Dad and Nate were toast.

"I don't think there's anything we can do," Dani said. "Not right at this moment, anyway. Luckily, we have some time to figure it out. The shuttle is going to take a day to reach Infinity Base. It's not a lot of time, but it's something."

Barely.

"We need to plan our own escape," said Mom.

"But—" I began.

She held up her index finger. "Gillian, we can't stay here. There's nothing in Eureka Cove for us, and every second we're here makes it more likely they'll find us." She turned to Dani. "When was the last time you slept?"

Dani rolled her eyes. "I gave up sleep when I was twenty. But maybe I'll take a shower. Don't know when I'll have another chance."

"Don't you want to chain us to the radiator or something before you go?" Eric asked drily.

Dani paused.

"My son is joking," Mom clarified. "We're not going to leave."

Dani still hesitated, watching us warily.

Mom threw her hands up in the air. "Please. I can't walk out of here with four kids in tow, and your stupid car won't work for me. We're not going anywhere without you. Take a shower!"

Wordlessly, Dani turned on her heel and departed.

Mom blew out a breath. "And here I thought your father was paranoid."

"You can't be paranoid if people are really after you," I quoted. Dad used to say that all the time. And he'd been right. People were after him—after all of us.

I gripped the photo album tightly. Dani's house was full of them. And Eric thought Dad's hobbies were weird. Growing up a Shepherd must have been beyond bizarre.

All Dani's pictures were with the same two or three people, and usually at least one of them was in a lab coat. Didn't she ever have any fun? I squinted at a shot of two kids running around in front of what looked like a rocket launch pad. The little brown girl with the beaded braids must have been Dani. The other kid was a white boy a few years older with dark hair styled in a bowl cut.

Savannah groaned in frustration and dropped the top of Howard's suit. "I don't think this is going to attach again. The loopy thing is warped from you chewing on it all summer," Savannah said. She held up the little pull. It was about the size of a dollar coin, but shaped like a hexagon. "Look, it's all twisted and broken." She squeezed it with her fingers, and it crumpled up like a paper fortune-teller into a little star-shaped pyramid.

"Well, what do you want me to do?" he asked. "Will you trade suits with me?"

"Ew, no," said Savannah. "Yours is disgusting."

Mom jumped up and started pacing back and forth, nervous energy pouring off her like a wake behind a boat.

Somehow, this scared me more than anything else that had happened today. We'd been in tough spaces before. I'd been trapped in a flooded underground city, holding my breath and swimming through tunnels until I thought my lungs would burst. I'd outrun a rocket ship.

But I didn't know what to do this time, and it didn't

look like the grown-ups did, either.

Eric looked at me, worried, and I knew he was think-ing the same thing as I was. We were in hiding from the Shepherds—*again*—and Mom was freaking out, just like when Dad made us hide off grid. I wished we could go back to just a few days ago, when all we had to worry about was whether we were going to move to Idaho and live with Mom.

Howard's forehead wrinkled. "But I want a complete suit."

Savannah sighed, taking pity on him, and reached for her own zipper pull. "Here, go get me a pair of scissors or something. You can have mine."

"Where am I supposed to find scissors?"

Abruptly, Eric stood up. "Come on. Dani's a com-puter engineer. She probably has wire cutters in her desk or something." They went off in search of tools.

Mom watched them go. "Well, that's one way to keep busy. The quest for the zipper pull." She turned to me. "How are you?"

"Scared," I answered honestly.

"Yeah," she agreed. She opened her mouth as if she was about to say something more—something stupid and untrue like *it's okay*—then thought better of it. "Yeah."

I toyed with the corner of the photo album I was hold-ing. "Nothing we've tried to do has worked. I let Dani knock us all out—I let her hurt Howard—and we're still stuck here."

"Oh, honey," Mom said, joining me on the couch. "You didn't let her hurt Howard. That was all on her."

But I was on a roll now. "And I don't know how we're going to get out of here. If we even raise our voices too loud her neighbors will hear us. We didn't get to Dad and Nate in time. And now we can't get to them at all."

"Gillian—"

"No, Mom," I said, my voice shaky. "I'm not stupid. They're in outer space. And Elana told me herself—she'll destroy Infinity Base before she lets Dr. Underberg escape again. We're not getting them back."

Mom sighed and put her arm around me. "No, you're not stupid. But your father wouldn't want you to give up, either. We can't trust Dani. But, Gillian, I do trust you."

I looked up at her.

"And I know that together we can think of a way out of here."

Dani emerged from her bedroom freshly washed. Her hair was done in a severe braid tucked down the back of her utility suit. "Where are the others?"

"In your office fixing a zipper pull."

Dani blinked. "Glad they're making themselves useful." She picked up the photo album from the couch cushions, where I'd left it. "Have you been researching my background, Gillian? You really are your father's daughter, aren't you?"

At least one of us was. I clenched my jaw. "What else did you want me to do?"

She examined the page I was on. "I remember this. It was one of our first test launches. We were all so excited."

"Who is that boy?" I asked, pointing at the dark-haired one doing a cartwheel on the launch pad.

"Believe it or not, that's Anton."

Anton Everett, the VP of Guidant. Anton Everett, killer of bees. I studied the skinny kid. He didn't look evil. He looked like someone I might see at school. Like someone I might even have been friends with. "I didn't realize he was so . . . young."

"He's five years older than me." She touched the photo gently for a second, then straightened. "I told you we grew up together."

Yeah, but hearing it and seeing them as kids were two entirely different things. I'd met Anton the day before yesterday, at that fancy dinner with Elana where he'd told us the world was ending and maybe the Shepherds had the right idea. If Anton was that devout a Shepherd, I doubted that he would be too thrilled with Dani tricking them all and hiding us. She really was giving up everything to help us escape.

"He's so brilliant," Dani said, as if lost in thought. "I've never met anyone like him, inside the Shepherds or outside. Unreal."

Mom was still watching Dani. "Your ex?"

"So obvious?" Dani said with a snort. She closed the album and tossed it aside. "Anton is obsessed with the end of the world. You can hardly have children with a man who thinks the human race is about to go extinct."

"No," Mom said. "The constant threat of disaster can make it difficult to raise a family."

I was sure she was talking about Dad now. Except we'd gone far beyond the threat of disaster this time.

The others emerged from Dani's office. Savannah and Eric took in our expressions and looked sufficiently worried. Howard toyed with his shiny new zipper pull. At least he wasn't chewing on it.

"How's your zipper, Howard?"

"Fine," he replied, as if the Shepherds hadn't just shot his brother into space. "The old one is broken, though." He held it up.

Dani leaned forward to take a look, then, unbelievably, started laughing.

She must have really gone around the bend this time. "What's wrong with you?"

"It's my father. He's so full of himself. His stupid riddles and his stupid codes. My mother used to say everything was a game to him. She was right. I just can't believe

I never noticed it before."

"What are you talking about?"

"I told you about my mother. She was a mathematician and a computer scientist." Dani retrieved the album and opened it to a page with a faded photograph of people in dorky-looking seventies clothes and hair. It was a lot of white guys and then Dani's mother—dark skin, bright eyes, hair done in a bouffant.

Savannah pointed out Dr. Underberg in the crowd. He looked so young, with broad shoulders and salt-and-pepper hair. "Is that where they fell in love?" she asked dreamily.

"More important, it's where Underberg got the idea to recruit her into the Shepherds," Dani replied. "We don't care about your race or your gender or your nationality."

"Yeah, Shepherds will lie to anyone," I said.

Dani ignored me. "She worked at NASA during the Apollo missions, just like Underberg. It kind of sucked for her back then. She was only twenty, and smarter than half the engineers on the projects. A perfect target for Shepherd recruitment. The falling in love or whatever . . . that happened later."

"Didn't your dad think the world was coming to an end, too?" I asked.

"Yes, but he's an optimist. He thinks we can save it. Omega City was meant to save us. And his version of Infinity Base was pure optimism. He thought the Shepherds' duty was to lead humanity to the stars."

Well, that sounded better than lying to them and then forcing them there, like the Shepherds did now.

She turned to another page in the album, this one showing her parents at some kind of cocktail party. They were seated together at a table, Dr. Underberg in a tuxedo, his hair much grayer, and Dani's mom beside him in a shimmery dress. Metallic streamers cascaded behind them, and there were shiny foil stars exploding out of a vase in the foreground of the shot. They were looking at the camera with uncertain smiles on their faces, as if caught unexpectedly during an intimate moment. "This is the only picture I have of the two of them. Not even the Shepherds knew they were together . . . until I was born, of course." She frowned, then shook it off. "See those things on the table?"

We all peered closer at the little figures scattered around the surface of the table. "What is it," I asked, "confetti?"

"They look like . . ." Savannah squinted. "Hexagons."

"Close," said Dani. "They're flexagons."

"What?" I asked.

"They're a mathematical puzzle," Dani said. "One of my mom's favorites. Have you heard of Möbius strips?"

"No," Eric, Howard, and I said.

"Yes," said Savannah. We all looked at her. "It's a strip of paper with only one side," she explained.

"Every piece of paper has two sides," Howard stated.

Dani leaned back. "Want to show them? There's some tape in my desk."

Savannah headed off, then returned with a notebook and a roll of Scotch tape. She pulled out a piece of paper, then tore it into a long ribbonlike strip, which she taped into a loop with a single twist in the middle. "This is a Möbius strip. It has only one side."

"No, it doesn't," Eric argued. "It has an inside and an outside."

"Wrong." Savannah handed it to him. "Try to color in just the outside."

Eric looked skeptical, but sat down at the coffee table and grabbed a pen. He started scribbling on the middle of the paper, starting at the piece of tape. He shifted the loop around as the colored-in parts got longer and longer, and when he got back to the piece of tape . . . the beginning of the scribbles weren't there.

"Oh. Where is it?" He frowned. "It's on the other side now."

"Keep going," said Savannah.

By the time Eric got back to the part where he'd first started coloring in the paper, the entire Möbius strip was completely covered in his scribbles.

Savannah folded her arms in triumph. "See? One side."

"Great," said Eric, tossing the strip at her. "What does that have to do with flexathingies?"

"Well," said Dani, "if a Möbius strip is a shape that has fewer sides than it should, then a flexagon is the opposite, a shape that has more sides than it should." She held up the zipper pull, flattened back out. "How many sides does this have, front and back?"

"Two," I said automatically.

Savannah's brow furrowed. She took it from Dani, letting it crumple up again into the arrowhead pyramid shape. The outside side was shiny, with the omega symbol raised like a ridge. The inside side—what had been the back side—was brushed silver. It didn't look anything like the Möbius strip. "Two?"

With the tip of her fingernail, Dani tugged at the peak of the pyramid, and the inside opened like a flower. Like magic, she flattened the shape out again. Now the brushed silver side was on top, and the shiny, omega-stamped side was on the bottom.

Savannah turned it over in her hand. The omega symbol was all messed up now, nothing but squiggles on the surface. "Weird," she said. "But still two."

"Do it again," Dani suggested.

Again, Savannah collapsed the hexagon into triangles, then, like Dani, she tugged at the peak of the pyramid.

This time what opened up was dark and grimy. I shuddered. This was what Howard had been sucking on for months.

But Savannah didn't look grossed out. She looked amazed. "Three!"

"Exactly." Dani grabbed a tissue and wiped it off. Underneath all the muck was another shiny surface, this one stamped with the crossed crooks-and-globe symbol of the Shepherds. "This is called a trihexaflexagon, because it has three sides and is shaped like a hexagon. There are lots of different kinds of hexaflexagons—some with six sides or even more. My mom loved these things."

"Wow," said Savannah. She kept folding it back and forth, revealing each of the three sides in turn. Howard stared intently at the piece of metal, gripping his own in his hand. He looked like he regretted trading with Savannah.

I touched the zipper pull on my own suit.

Eric made a face. "Why would he put a puzzle on a zipper pull?"

"That's Underberg for you," Dani said. "It's not remotely practical, but he was always doing that. Little games and puzzles and stuff for his friends. And the people he made the utility suits for were definitely his friends."

"True," I said. "That's how we found Omega City in the first place. Only people who knew him could have figured out the riddle in his diary."

"And my code book," Howard said. "We never could have figured out those codes if he hadn't sent me that code book from outer space."

Dani frowned. "I'm still not certain how he did that. Or why."

Was she serious? "It's so we could figure out the messages you were sending," I argued. "So we could find out all the fishy stuff going on around here and try to stop it."

"Wouldn't it have been easier to send a note saying that there was a lot of fishy stuff going on around here?" Savannah asked. "You know, before we put ourselves in all this danger?"

"No," Mom said, her voice tight. "That would have been *helpful*. But this is a game. And he played it with children." She sounded like she had back before the divorce. We'd been hiding out from the Shepherds then, too, in a tent in the woods. And just like then, there hadn't been a thing she could do about it.

"Dr. Underberg clearly thinks very highly of your children, Grace," said Dani.

"Yeah," Eric said, rolling his eyes. "The guy thought it would be fun to take us into outer space in his broken-down rocket. The guy who just had a rocket sitting around ready to get shot into outer space in the first place. He's crazy. We're lucky we're not all melted puddles of goo at the bottom of the Omega City missile silo."

Dani turned to him, her eyes wide. "That's it. That's how we'll get to Dr. Underberg."

"What?" Eric asked. "Goo?"

"No," she replied. "Omega City."

"Omega City was destroyed."

"But the ruins were taken over by the Shepherds. Remember, Eric?" I said. "Dad took us back to the site and they had all those barbed-wire fences up?" Dad had tried to look into the company that bought out the land where Omega City lay buried, but he'd never been able to uncover much about them. It was a Shepherd front.

"We've been excavating the ruins for months," Dani said. "That's why I have the extra utility suit I wore, and the one I gave to you, Dr. Seagret."

"So if we can get to Omega City, you think you can send a message to Dr. Underberg?" I asked as a spark of hope ignited inside me.

"I can do better than that, Gillian. If we can get to Omega City, then I can save them all."

6

UFO

AT LEAST WE DIDN'T HAVE TO GO BACK INSIDE THE PODS. I MEAN, IT didn't feel better at the moment, sardined inside the trunk of Dani's car with my mother, Eric, Savannah, and Howard, but I tried to look on the bright side: I was conscious, and I wasn't trapped in the dark alone.

"Does anyone want to sing a song?" Eric asked from near my elbow. "Play a game? I Spy?"

"Shut up, Eric," said Savannah from somewhere near my knee.

"I spy with my little eye, something black."

"What shape is it?" Howard asked. He was up behind Eric somewhere.

"Has to be a yes or no question," Eric said.

"Um . . . is it round?"

"I can't tell," Eric said, cracking himself up. "I can't see a thing."

"Shut up!" Savannah and I shouted.

"Girls!" scolded Mom, down near the taillights.

No one would hear us, with the possible exception of Dani herself.

"Sorry," Eric said, though he didn't sound it. "I was just trying to find a way to pass the time that didn't involve wondering who it was that farted."

"Eww!" said Savannah. "It was probably you."

"Probably," admitted Eric. "So, want to play Punch Buggy?"

"I'm going to punch *you*," I said. I wiggled my arm so he could see I was capable of it. Well, not *see*, but tell.

"Fine," he grumbled. "We can lie here in silence all the way to Omega City."

I'd planned to spend the trip going over Dani's plan in my head, repeating it so I knew where we were, even from inside the trunk, and could figure out if things were proceeding the way they should or if this, too, was going to turn into a massive mess.

Once you're all loaded in the car, it should take about ten minutes for us to drive to the edge of the resident portion of the Eureka Cove campus.

We had to have been in the car for more than ten minutes by now, right? I'd lost count somewhere around two hundred fifty Mississippi. Didn't she have to stop at the security gate and talk to a guard? Maybe not, given that she was a Shepherd.

From there, we'll head straight to the helipad. If we time it right, it should be between guard shifts. With any luck, my executive-level clearance should help me bypass the necessary authorizations for both the release of the helicopter and the logging of our flight plan.

This was the part I was most nervous about. I didn't think anyone would bother Dani if she was just driving in a car through Guidant. But Dani taking off in a helicopter for points unknown? People noticed helicopters. Still, she assured us it was the quickest way to Omega City.

And we were definitely under a time crunch. We only had twenty hours before the Shepherd shuttle reached Infinity Base. We had to get to Omega City, get inside, and find a way to contact Dr. Underberg before he fell for the Shepherds' trap.

"That's weird," said Savannah a minute later.

"What?" I asked, wriggling a bit to look in her general direction.

"Ow, Gills. Your elbows," said Eric.

"Nothing," said Sav. "I just keep playing with the hexaflexagon, and I thought for a second I felt another side. But it's gone now."

"How can you tell in the dark?"

"Well, the shiny omega side is smooth, right? And the brushed side is ridged. And the hidden side, with the Shepherd symbol, is all dirty and stuff, so it feels gritty."

"Let me feel." I reached down.

"Gills!" said Eric. "Elbows!"

I'd show him elbows.

Savannah carefully handed me the tiny zipper pull, and I did that squeeze-and-fold movement I'd seen her do to turn the hexaflexagon inside out, over and over. Smooth, ridged, gritty. Smooth ridged, gritty. Smooth, ridged, bumpy . . . wait. Bumpy?

"Whoa!" I said, running my fingers over the pebbly surface. "You're right."

"Dani said sometimes they had more sides," Howard pointed out.

"What is it?" Eric said, crowding up on me.

"It's another side."

He jostled me again, and the zipper pull went flying out of my fingers.

"Eric!" I felt around on the carpeted floor of the trunk. "Where is it?"

"Did you lose it?" Savannah asked.

"It was Eric's fault."

"Was not!"

"Eric, Gillian," Mom warned.

I kept patting the carpet, expecting to feel the edges of the metal.

"Let me look," said Howard. "I have my flashlight." He shifted to pull it out of his cargo pocket and kneed Eric, whose head knocked into mine. Hard.

"Ow!" we cried.

There was another large bump, then a shuddering around us, as if we were coming to a halt. Everyone went very still, and very, very quiet.

"Hello, Miss Alcestis," said a voice, muffled, by the pass-through into the car. "Did you schedule the helicopter this afternoon? I don't have anything on the log."

"Oh, that's funny." Dani's voice. "Should be on there. Can you get it ready for departure?"

"Sure. Go ahead and park and I'll get her set up for you."

The car moved again, slowly and with loud scraping sounds, as if driving over gravel.

"The guard will complicate matters," she said. "I need you all to stay perfectly still until I get you, and then you need to move as fast as possible onto the helicopter."

"Got it," said Howard, and his flashlight flicked on. I bit my lip. Wasn't he even listening?

Mom covered the light with her hand. "Not now, Howard," she whispered.

More silence. More waiting. I turned up the cooling setting on my suit as the air in the trunk became stuffy. We heard the guard return, and he and Dani had a short discussion about the helicopter. Her door opened and she got out. More silence. More waiting.

Then the trunk door opened and we all squinted into the bright light. Dani stood over us, her face set in stern lines.

"Now."

We all scrambled to sit up and scoot out of the trunk. My muscles ached from being cramped up so long, but I ignored them and followed my mom and Howard out of the car. Eric followed but Savannah was still inside, kneeling on the floor and feeling around for her zipper pull.

"Savannah, now," Mom said.

"Coming!" She ran her fingers across the fibers.

"No, now." Mom grabbed her arm and tugged.

Savannah leaned over and plucked something off the carpet. "Got it."

I turned around, trying to get my bearings. We were standing on a small gravel lot near a low building. Nearby was a large asphalt pad with a helicopter sitting in the center like a great glass dragonfly. And near the door of the building lay the guard in a crumpled heap.

Mom turned to Dani, her eyes wide with terror. "What did you do to him?"

Dani shrugged and started toward the helicopter, herding us along. "I tranqued him."

"What?" Mom shrieked.

"There was no other way." She pulled open the glass door of the helicopter and ushered us aboard.

"You said you wouldn't do that anymore!" Mom insisted. The four kids all crowded into the back of the helicopter, while Mom sat down in the copilot seat, still glaring hard at Dani.

Dani climbed inside and shut the door. "Dr. Seagret, as you are so fond of pointing out, I'm a Shepherd. We lie."

Mom just folded her arms and glared. I looked at the guard through the plexiglass sides of the helicopter, trying desperately to feel any of Mom's outrage. But the guard had been a Shepherd. Maybe even one of the Shepherds that had attacked Mom and Nate the other day.

Besides, what other option did we have? It was us or Them.

I wondered if the Shepherds felt the same way. When Dad wrote his book on Underberg and got close to exposing the Shepherds' past and they'd retaliated by destroying his career and our family, it was us or Them, too. Dani said we all learned right from wrong, we just learned different rights and different wrongs, and the further it went, the more it seemed as if their rights were the complete opposite of ours, until everything, even our lives, came to be about us or Them. Until I could look at a man lying in the road and think it was okay because it meant we escaped detection.

Which I guess made me not so very different from the Shepherds.

Dani reached up to a little hook in the roof of the copter and pulled down a headset with big half-sphere earphones the size of softballs and turned to us. "Shoulder harnesses on and locked in, guys. Over each of your seats, you'll find a headset. You'll need these during flight, not just so you can hear each other, but also to protect your ears from the sound of the machinery. Put them on, and lower the attached boom mic so you can speak into them."

We did as we were told. The headsets were thick and heavy, and attached to the helicopter via power cable. They must have come equipped with some sort of noise-canceling technology, for when I put them on, not only did everything go quiet and muffled, but there was a distinct, tinny not-sound in my ears, like a television set to an empty channel.

"Is everyone ready?" Dani's voice buzzed in my ear.

"I suppose this is the wrong time to ask how much experience you have flying a helicopter?" Mom's voice was dry as she questioned Dani.

"Yes," replied Dani, as I felt rather than heard the whoop-whoop of the blades beginning to spin above my head. "It is."

As we lifted from the ground, my stomach seemed to sink into my lap. This was nothing like flying in a plane. The plexiglass sides made it seem like we were just floating up here, despite the rhythmic roar of the blades. I leaned over to look as the ground receded beneath us. Already the security guard looked more like a squashed bug on the lawn than a person.

"Ahem. Sit straight back there, unless you want us to tip," Dani's voice barked in my ear.

I shot back against the seat. *Tip?* "You're kidding, right?" I breathed into the microphone.

"No," Dani said. "Now stop talking. This is harder than it looks."

Savannah grabbed my hand and squeezed as we rose into the sky.

AFTER A WHILE, Dani seemed to relax. Maybe it was when we reached a cruising altitude, or we got well past the confines of Eureka Cove. Below us, the ground spread out like a bumpy green carpet. Without shifting too much in my seat, I was mesmerized by the sight of the Earth below us. We were flying steadily west as the afternoon sun shone brightly into the cabin.

"Twelve times," Dani said, breaking a fifteen-minute silence. "I've flown a helicopter twelve times."

"Cool." Eric's voice broke through on the headset. "We've ridden in one once. Now."

Dani chuckled. "Every Shepherd is required to get training in multiple types of aircraft. I have certifications in small craft, jets, rotorcraft, paraplanes, and lighter-than-air . . ."

"What's lighter-than-air?" Howard asked.

"Dirigibles. You know, blimps."

"Why do you do that?" I asked. "You won't need blimps in outer space."

"No, but the training is important, and different skill sets build on one another. For instance, I know much more about moving around in zero gravity because of all my pilot training."

"How many times have you been to outer space?" Howard asked.

"Not twelve," Dani said. "I don't share the fondness for it that Anton does. Or Dr. Underberg, for that matter. But we all have our strengths. My gift is computers. I've also done a lot of advanced physical training as well—martial arts, meditation, endurance—pushing the human body to its limits and beyond."

I remembered her wild cliff dive back on the island.

"So how do you become a Shepherd?" Howard asked.

"I mean, what if you wanted to join?"

"Howard!" I cried.

"I mean, what if they didn't hate us or whatever. Or got over it?" Howard looked at me, as if confused by my reaction. "Or something?"

"You'd join the Shepherds just to go into outer space?" Savannah asked in disbelief.

"You bet I would," he replied.

Dani laughed again. "Well, I guess that would depend on the person," she said as we flew on and the sky began to darken around us. "I was born a Shepherd. There was really no other option for me. My mother was recruited because she wasn't getting to do the kind of work she wanted at NASA. And Dr. Underberg was the same. He thought the government was wasting time fighting wars when we could focus instead on human progress that would make the very reasons for those wars—fights over land or resources— obsolete. Think about it: If every human being had a new planet to live on, or endless energy, or all the wealth of a solar system, who would we fight? And why?"

There were times when Dani sounded almost normal. When all the Shepherds did. When they talked about the vast potential of humanity, and the glorious future that awaited us if we all worked together for our own good. Then they killed bees and kidnapped people's fathers and pretended that asteroids were going to destroy the Earth to hide the fact that they'd built a secret space station, and you remembered how bonkers it all was.

Howard slumped. "So I'd have to become a famous scientist first?"

"You won't want to be a Shepherd, Howard," I said, balling my hands into fists. "Especially not after I'm done with them."

"They aren't so bad," Dani said. "I know it doesn't seem that way right now . . ."

"Right now, when we're running for our lives?" said Mom. "No, it doesn't."

Dani kept speaking over her. "But it was an amazing way to grow up. Shepherds take children seriously, you know. That wasn't an act, this weekend at Eureka Cove. They really are very impressed with the children and the fortitude and imagination they displayed in Omega City. If things had gone differently, maybe you would all be Shepherds right now, and none of this would have been necessary."

"When would things have had to start going differently?" Mom asked. "Back before you ruined my husband's career? Because I'll tell you right now, that was the last possible moment that he would have even considered working with you people."

"Yeah!" I exclaimed. "Go, Mom!"

Mom actually turned around in her seat to smirk at me. Eric looked shocked.

"If there were no Shepherds," Dani pointed out, "there would have been no Omega City."

"If there were no Shepherds," I said, "then maybe you would have grown up knowing your father."

"Or maybe I never would have been born," she snapped back.

There was a long silence, and the sound of the engine and the chop-chop-chop of the helicopter blades did little to fill it.

"I know that you made a huge sacrifice for us today," Mom said, "and no matter our disagreements, we're more grateful than we can possibly express, aren't we, kids?"

"Yes," we all said. I added under my breath, "But I still wouldn't want to be a Shepherd."

"Oh, I would!" Howard said. I was mortified—did everyone hear me? Stupid mic! "They send you to space, they teach you how to fly a helicopter. Eric, you should have seen Dani dive off that cliff. It was so cool!"

"You dove off a cliff?" Mom asked her.

"Thanks for sticking up for me, Howard," Dani said. "Gillian, I understand your perspective. If I were you, I would feel the same way. Actually, I do feel the same way. That's what I'm doing here."

I thought about Dani's home. The pictures on the walls and in the photo albums. Her mother was dead. She'd never met her dad. She no longer believed in the cause she was raised to serve. My father was right now in a spaceship somewhere far above my head, too, but I knew him and loved him. Mom and Eric were a few feet away, as well as my two best friends in the whole wide world. I had everyone. Who did Dani have?

"Sorry," I said.

Dani's back was very straight in the front seat as she flew on. "Thanks."

The sun was low in the sky now, shining directly at us. Howard zipped up the hood and visor on his utility suit, and after squinting into the glare for a bit, the rest of us did the same. We must have made quite a sight—six silver-encased creatures in a big glass bubble. If anyone on the ground caught a picture, we could be the subject of one of my father's alien classes.

I wondered if Dad would be teaching classes ever again. My eyes began to sting.

Even if we managed to open up a channel of communication with Dr. Underberg in Omega City, there was no guarantee he'd be able to save my father and Nate. Dani believed that if we could really talk to him—have a conversation, and not just a few stilted, coded messages—we'd be able to convince him to negotiate with Elana for the safe return of Dad and Nate. It would, however, require him to compromise his principles when it came to the Shepherds and their lies. Every time I considered that, there was a small, hard place inside me that screamed *Never!* I knew that place was inside Dr. Underberg, too.

And for him, I feared it was the only thing that mattered.

ALPHA AND OMEGA

AS THE HELICOPTER CRESTED THE LAST OF THE TREES AND DESCENDED slowly into the open field, a strange thrill stole through me. The last time I'd seen this place it was a smoldering wasteland—acres of charred grass and sandy earth melted into a glassy crust. Nate's truck had been a twisted hunk of metal, and the scene had been lit by the colored, flashing lights of cop cars and fire trucks.

Now it was as if none of that had ever occurred. The field was a neatly mowed lawn of slightly yellowed summer grass. The fence around the perimeter was tall and topped with a generous swirl of razor-sharp barbed wire, but that was obviously no obstacle to the helicopter. There was a small road cutting through the pasture, which led to a single, lonely cinder-block building with a corrugated tin roof that glinted orange in the light of the setting sun. The place seemed deserted.

Next stop: *Omega City*.

Dani maneuvered the helicopter toward the ground, concentrating intently as we bobbed and dipped. She was aiming for a relatively flat patch of grass near the building, but clearly wary of skimming too close to the structure with our blades. I clenched my jaw as we jolted and slid into a landing.

"Sorry." She cut off the engine and lifted her headset. "Need more than twelve flights' worth of practice to stick the landing."

One by one, we spilled out of the helicopter. I pulled back my hood and took a deep breath. The air smelled dusty, like old fires. Or maybe that was only my imagination. The Shepherds had long ago bulldozed the burnt remains of trees and turned over all the earth. Of course, rocket fuel was probably always hazardous to your health. I kicked at the grass.

Mom looked around, her face creased with worry. "This is more remote than I was expecting. Maybe we'd better take the children to a safe location first."

Dani blinked at her and crossed her arms. "Where are you suggesting?"

"A police station?"

She rolled her eyes. "And again, I ask how you're going to explain this to them. Do you really think they're going to let me just walk out of there after I fly a stolen Guidant helicopter into their parking lot? That they aren't going to call Guidant first thing to try to get to the bottom of this? If we go to the police, we've lost any chance of contacting Underberg."

"Okay, then what about the Nolands' house? We could leave the children there."

"Sure," Dani said, sarcastic. *"Hey, Mr. and Mrs. Noland, can you babysit these guys for a while? We have to go rescue your son Nate from the evil scientists who shot him into space.* That'll be a quick conversation."

"No, it won't," said Howard matter-of-factly.

Mom rubbed the heels of her hands over her forehead. "There has to be an option. This is madness. I can't— they're *children*. The last time they were here, they almost drowned."

"I'd say Omega City is in much better shape now," Dani said.

"And so are we," Savannah pointed out. "My arm's fine, and Eric's teeth are fixed."

"Yeah," said Eric. "Besides, this time at least we're with grown-ups. I don't want you to leave us with people who don't know what's going on, Mom."

I chimed in, too. "Remember what they did to you and Nate at Guidant? At least if the Shepherds come back, we're prepared for whatever they want to do to us. The Nolands wouldn't be."

Dani sighed, and slung a bulky bag over her shoulder. "We're wasting time. The longer we stand here talking, the less chance we have to do *anything* before Guidant figures out where we've gone."

Mom turned to us and took a deep breath. "I'm saying this now, because I might not have the opportunity later. If the Shepherds come back, if anyone comes after us, you guys run and hide. Understand?"

I didn't really want to point this out to Mom, but that's what we always did. That's how we'd ended up in Omega City to start with. That's what we'd done at every juncture on the island at Eureka Cove. At a certain point, running and hiding wasn't going to solve anything. But we all nodded anyway. It was the only way to move along.

Dani started toward the building. "Follow me."

The building ahead of us was about the size of an ice-cream stand. No power or telephone cables ran to it, and though small windows were spaced evenly around the exterior, I couldn't see anything inside. The door featured a keypad and one of those tablet-sized panels I recognized from Eureka Cove. Dani paused here, dropped her bag to the ground, and unzipped it. Inside, I could see what looked like some electronic equipment, and even the corner of one of her own photo albums. I leaned in for a better look and she glared at me and snatched the edges closed. She pulled out a small gray box with a port at one end, opened the panel near the bottom of the tablet, and inserted the plug.

The screen flickered on with the imprint of a palm.

Welcome, Anton Everett came from the speaker.

She yanked the box back out of the port as the door unlocked, and didn't meet any of our eyes. We followed her inside to a small, plain room with a desk, a few chairs, and some computer monitors showing different scenes from the yard, the road, the gate near the fence, and some empty corridors. One whole wall was a large silver piece of sheet metal. Dani stopped dead in the middle of the floor and scanned the room.

"Where to, Anton Everett?" Mom drawled.

"I guess . . ." Dani frowned, staring at the wall. "Give me a minute." She crossed to the desk and plugged her little box into a port there. Once again, Anton Everett's log-in information came up.

"This looks like a giant elevator door," Howard said, staring at the silver wall. "But there's no button."

"That must be a huge disappointment for you," said Savannah. She had the hexaflexagon zipper pull back in her hands and was rotating it through its sides again. "I don't get it," she mumbled. "It was just here a second ago . . ."

"Why are you logged in as Anton?" I asked Dani as she sat at the desk and pulled up a file on the screen marked "Access Codes."

"Because they're supposed to think I'm still at Eureka Cove," she said, not looking up from the monitor. "Got it."

"But won't Anton wonder why he's suddenly showing up here?"

"That's why we're going to be quick."

There was a rumbling behind me, and I whirled around to see the silver wall sliding away to reveal a large, concrete cargo elevator.

"Everyone in," said Dani. "Let's go."

We dutifully boarded the elevator. The doors rumbled closed. There were no buttons inside, but after a moment, I could tell we were moving down.

Howard bounced up and down with excitement.

"How long does it take?" Mom asked, her hands clasped tightly in front of her.

"A while," said Eric. "If last time is anything to go by."

"But this is a new elevator," I said. "Guidant built this recently. I'm sure it's quicker . . . right, Dani?"

Dani just looked at a place above the door, where usually you'd see a floor display, and gripped the handle of her bag.

"Are you okay?" I asked her. Sometimes I got a little nervous in elevators, too. Especially since Omega City. But

Dani was a pilot. She'd been in space.

"Found it," Savannah announced. She held up the zipper pull. "See? Another side. A bumpy one."

"Let me see." Eric reached for the piece of metal. "How do you do it?"

"Pinch two of the triangles next to each other together, and then fold the opposite ones down. . . ." She showed him, closing her hands around his. "Wait . . . what did you do?"

He yanked his fingers back. "What? What did I do?"

"It's *another* side!" She shook her head in disbelief and ran her fingertip across the uncovered surface.

"A hexahexaflexagon," said Dani absentmindedly. "Well, never let it be said that Underberg doesn't overdo things—"

There was a small jolt as the elevator halted. The doors slid open, and all talk of zipper pulls ceased.

Before us lay the main chamber of Omega City. But it was Omega City like I'd never seen it before. The last time I was here, the chamber was dark and flooded, with collapsed buildings and rusty, rickety walkways. Now everything was clean and repaired. Blue-white light illuminated the cavern like the inside of a sports stadium, and I could see for the first time how large the space truly was. Everything sparkled and shimmered, and the buildings had all been freshly painted. I imagined this was what it looked like when Dr. Underberg first built it, although instead of the old red omega symbol, all the doors and walls were marked with the globe and crossed crooks of the Shepherds.

"Wow," said Mom. "This is even nicer than I expected. In Sam's book, it sounded a little sketchy."

"It wasn't like this," Savannah assured her. "Everything was broken. And wet."

"Mrs. Dr. S!" said Howard to Mom. "Mrs. Dr. S. That's where they shot at us!" He pointed at the base of the stability springs. Each coiled round was bigger than a car. I remembered Dad explaining that the buildings were positioned on springs to help them remain stable in case of a direct nuclear attack.

"And there's where the grain storage and the greenhouse was." The old buildings had been razed, and a new structure in that location looked a bit like the biostation under Eureka Cove—a large, bubbly dome, glowing faintly red.

"And over there was the entrance to the missile silo." He pointed at a door across the cavern covered in construction scaffolding.

"Where are we headed?" I asked Dani.

But she said nothing, just stared. The bag dropped from her arms and clunked on the concrete floor.

"Dani?" Mom said.

She swallowed, and her eyes glistened. "The pictures don't do it justice. All this . . . all this."

"Wait," I said, suddenly realizing why she'd been so quiet. "You've never been here?"

She seemed to catch herself and looked away, swiping her bag off the ground. "It's not my area. Not many computers around here. At least, not the kind that can't be hacked by a five-year-old with a cell phone."

"But you didn't even come, just to see?" I asked, amazed. "Your father built this place!"

She turned left, then right, then left again. "This way, I think."

"She *thinks*?" Eric echoed, incredulous. "Great, just what I need, to get lost here again." He trotted after her.

I ran to catch up. "Why didn't you want to see it?"

"Lots of people built this place, Gillian," she said coldly as she marched along. "It wasn't just Underberg down here with a hammer and some nails." She approached a door marked *Staircase 3: Training, Medical Offices, Communication.* "Here we are." She went inside and started taking the stairs two at a time.

I raced after her, heedless of whether the others were following behind or still giving my mother the tour. "Yeah, but it was his baby. His entirely after the Shepherds tried to destroy it, and him. He *lived* here. For ages. Weren't you curious? Didn't you want to find out more about what he was doing all those years?"

Dani ran faster. She had almost a foot on me, and had done all those wacky physical training regimens the Shepherds taught, but I didn't give up, even when she got so far ahead of me I couldn't hear her feet on the stairs.

I didn't understand her at all. If I'd found out my father had spent years hiding out somewhere, I would definitely have wanted to see it. Plus, it was a Shepherd project. It didn't make any sense.

I heard another door open, high above me, and sprinted up the last flight of stairs.

The corridor looked familiar, and then I remembered. This was the way to the communications room, the central nerve center of Omega City. This was where I'd fought with Fiona and refused to surrender. This was where I'd first seen the videos of Dr. Underberg arguing for the importance of saving mankind. I stood there for a moment, catching my breath and getting my bearings. I hadn't given in the last time I was here. I wasn't going to do it now.

The door to the communications room was ajar, and I saw Dani's bag lying on the floor inside. I pushed the door wide and saw her seated at a desk. The video library with its neat, hand-lettered messages, which once had made the room seem crowded and cramped, was entirely gone now, replaced by large servers and other electronic equipment. The giant control panel was still there, with its map of Omega City, paths of colored lights, and millions of switches, but it was now covered with enormous pieces of plexiglass, over which was suspended a large touch-screen monitor that replicated the patterns on the analog panel below. Dani plugged her little hacking device into this monitor and got to work.

Again a palm print flashed on the screen; again the computer spoke another person's name. "Anton Everett. Security access granted."

All of a sudden, I understood everything. Why she was using Anton's identity, why she didn't know her way around Omega City . . . why she was helping us at all.

"You've never been here before," I said, still panting a bit from my haste to catch her, "because you weren't allowed."

Silence. Dani kept working. "Yes, you're very intelligent, Gillian. As you know."

But not smart enough to have figured her out before she brought us this far.

"You weren't allowed," I went on, "because they didn't know if they could trust you to see this place and not feel a connection to your father."

"In which matter," she replied, as calmly as ever, "they were clearly correct." She stopped working for a second, and her lips pursed. "You know what this place is. What it meant to him. He built this for humanity. He built it for my mother, and for me, and for everyone he ever loved. He disagreed with the Arkadia Group that it should be kept secret from humanity, that everything they did should be kept secret—and they retaliated."

Then, just as now, it was more important for the Shepherds to keep their secrets than to do right by the human race. They might talk about looking to the stars, but their corporate arms seemed to have their eyes on the bottom line. First the Arkadia Group, then Guidant Technologies. They weren't afraid to destroy what they'd built, destroy Dr. Underberg, to protect themselves.

I remembered what Elana had said on the phone.

We have to protect Guidant, even if that means sacrificing Infinity Base.

And I still had questions.

"They've been working on Omega City for ten months. You've read my father's book and seen what Dr. Underberg was trying to do here. If you can hack into Shepherd security and come here whenever you want, why didn't you?"

She swiveled around in her seat and met my eyes. "I never had a reason to risk my place with the Shepherds before. Right or wrong, they're my family, not Dr. Underberg."

I shook my head. "But you don't think they're wrong, do you? You never did."

She turned back to her machines, all business again.

"Of course I did. I told you so."

She did. But Shepherds lie.

"*When* did you decide they were wrong?" I pressed. "It wasn't when Anton genetically engineered bees to die. It wasn't when the Shepherds tried to ruin the career of an innocent history professor. It wasn't even when they kidnapped Mom and Dad and Nate. I saw you that afternoon, on the cliff. You told me to run, but you didn't try to help." I heard the others in the corridor behind me.

"I think this is where they went," Eric was saying.

"You'd know better than me" came Savannah's voice. "I only got here through the air vents."

"Right," said Mom. She sounded overwhelmed.

I only had a few seconds to get this out. "You weren't interested in helping us or saving us then. That wasn't enough to risk your position with the Shepherds."

"You're right. It wasn't."

"And what was?" I went on, although I thought I already knew.

"When Elana told me she planned to kill my father."

This was the answer I was waiting for, but it still felt as if a big metal hand was squeezing my heart.

She swiveled around and fixed me with a glare. "I'd do anything to stop that. I'm sure you understand." Then she went back to work.

Yes, I did understand. I didn't like it one little bit, but I understood it perfectly. I was doing the same thing. Elana had threatened my father, and I'd let Dani tranquilize me and stick me in a pod. I'd talked my mother into letting us come to Omega City. I'd followed Dani no matter how worried I got that she had no idea what she was doing, no matter how strange or untrustworthy she acted. Because she was the only one who was willing to tell me that we could save Dad.

"Hey, guys," Eric said, when the four of them reached the threshold. "What's up? Did you guys get hold of Dr. Underberg yet?"

"No," I said without taking my eyes off Dani. She didn't look up from her work to greet them, either.

Honestly, I wasn't even sure if we *could* get in touch with Dr. Underberg from here. Because if all Dani had to do was pick up a phone from Omega City and call him, why go to the trouble of sending out her stupid number codes? She said she hadn't been willing to risk her job until the Shepherds threatened to kill him, but if she could just hack into the system and pretend to be someone else whenever she wanted, why hadn't she done so a long time ago?

Had she brought us all here—had *I* brought us all here—only to get smacked in the face with more lies?

"How long will this take?" Mom asked. "I'm beginning to get worried about staying here. It's too dangerous."

"You're right, Mom." It was dangerous. I just wanted

to find out how much danger we were in. I realized now that though Dani had promised to contact Dr. Underberg, she hadn't exactly told us how.

"I'm right?" Mom laughed. "Never thought I'd hear that from you, honey."

Dani frowned, looking at the screen. "Well, that's going to be trouble."

"What?" Mom asked.

Dani tapped the screen, where an orange alert flashed.
Personnel: Security Check Required.

"What is it?" I asked.

"They want us to call in and verify our identities," Dani said. "They're onto us."

KNOWLEDGE VERSUS WISDOM

"WE OBVIOUSLY CAN'T DO THAT," SAID MOM. "RIGHT? I MEAN, CAN YOUR little box thingy do anything to pretend you're . . . who-ever?" She gestured to the device Dani had been using to hack all the computers in Omega City.

"Anton Everett," said Dani. "And it would be some-thing of a challenge. I have enough recordings of him to make a voice model, but I don't have access to the program we use from here, and I don't know if I could even make a model in time to appease them.

"What happens if we don't respond?" Mom asked.

"They might lock down the whole facility. They'll

definitely be sending people in to check on us. The clock is ticking."

"The clock is ticking for *what*?" I pressed. I wasn't letting go until I had answers. "To call Dr. Underberg?"

"What?" said Dani. "Oh. Yes."

"Why would he pick up now?"

"Excuse me?"

"If you could always call Dr. Underberg from Omega City, then the Shepherds must have tried, right? Sometime in the last ten months? And he wasn't interested in talking to them."

"Well, yes," said Dani, "but this time it's *me* . . ."

"How would he know that?" I asked. "If you could pretend to be anyone."

Dani sighed. "Okay. Fine. I wasn't planning on calling him from Omega City."

There it was. I looked at the others, but the significance of her words didn't seem to have sunk in.

"Then where were you going to call him from?" Mom asked.

Dani turned back to the screen, where the security alert still blinked, and tapped a portion of the map marked *Restricted Area*. "From there."

We leaned in to look. The map of Omega City sometimes felt like it was permanently marked on my brain, but I wasn't familiar with this section. We hadn't traveled through it on our first visit, but it looked familiar to me, even so.

"It's a silo," I whispered.

"*Another* silo?" Eric said.

And Howard put it together. "Another rocket ship?"

A thrill coursed through me as I realized her plan. A second rocket ship. Another way to get to space. To get to Dad.

"Oh dear," said Savannah.

"Wait." Mom held up her hands. "You brought us here to get on one of Dr. Underberg's rocket ships? Are you delusional?"

"No one said *you* had to get on," Dani replied. "I'm getting on. I'm going into space and I'm going to find my father and bring him home." She pressed another key and the screen went dark. "And, if you help me, I'll bring home Dr. Seagret and Nate, too. There's no way Dr. Underberg can do that on his own. He was an old man before he went into space. He'll need help. My help."

We all stood there for a moment, letting it sink in. On one hand, I understood why she hadn't told us the truth earlier. Mom definitely wouldn't have signed on for a rocket-ship launch, given that the last one had nearly killed us all.

But on the other hand, Dani was right. If we wanted to save Dad and Nate, we were going to have to do more than just *call* Dr. Underberg. What could he do, anyway? He was an old man, and going alone to Infinity Base would just be playing into the Shepherds' hands.

On the other hand, Dani, with her piloting experience and cliff diving know-how and quick trigger on the tranquilizer—well, she was probably better equipped than anyone to actually rescue Dad and Nate. Once she got into space.

"I don't . . . ," Mom said, flustered. "I can't . . . how would that even work? You can't just launch a rocket into space like you're taking your car out for a drive."

"Why not?" Dani said. "Underberg did it, and his rocket ship was in far worse shape than ours. His whole city was. I'm a much more experienced pilot than he is, too. Not that there needs to be much piloting. I'll program the flight path in advance, so basically all piloting will take care of itself." She looked at her watch. "That is, if we manage to get to the rocket before security shows up. The clock is ticking. Either you trust me to do this and you'll help me, or you don't, and we should all just surrender now."

Mom glared at her. "That is an incredibly unfair thing to say. You put us in this situation without all the information, and now you're holding it over us?"

"I beg your pardon, Dr. Seagret," Dani replied, "but did you really have an alternative?"

Mom stood very still for a long moment while we all

looked at her. Somehow, I resisted the urge to clasp my hands in front of me and beg, but if my face was anything like Eric's, I didn't need to.

There was no other option. And there was no choice, either—not really. Not if we wanted to save Dad's and Nate's lives. And there wasn't a single person in the room who was willing to walk away from that.

"How do we get to the other rocket?" Howard asked abruptly.

"Wait a second," Mom said, holding out her arms as if to keep us from rushing off. "You guys aren't going any-where. I read *The Forgotten Fortress*, remember? I know what happens to those silos when the rocket launches. They burn up. You're staying right here."

"Where the security guards can get us?" Savannah asked, then hesitated. "Actually, that's a good point. After you blast into outer space, where are we supposed to hide?"

Dani grimaced.

"Great, she hasn't thought through this part, either." Eric groaned and pushed past her toward the map. "Excuse me while I look up the Omega City Panic Room."

"So this is an escape . . . for you." Mom folded her arms. "We're going to end up exactly where we started."

"You could come into space with me," Dani suggested.

"Yes!" Howard nodded vigorously.

"Pass," insisted Mom. "Hard pass."

"Then where do we go?" Howard asked. "Everyone gets to go into space but me!"

"Don't worry, Howard," said Savannah. "I'm not going into space."

"My brother, Dani. Everyone." He folded up the hood of his suit, I guess in protest.

But I didn't have time to worry about hurting Howard's feelings. "We do need a place to hide."

"This was supposed to be your place to hide," Dani admitted. "At least until I eliminated the threat up there." She tapped her foot. "We're running out of time. If I don't get to that rocket soon, I won't be able to save any of you."

"I appreciate that," said my mother. "But my priority is these children. I can't let them fall into the wrong hands. There's no knowing what the Shepherds might do if they find us here. They might—" She stopped herself from completing that thought. But we could all figure out what she was going to say.

They might even kill us.

Dani considered this. "Okay. Then call the police."

"What?" Mom said. "I thought you said calling the police wasn't going to do any good. That they'd never believe us about what the Shepherds were doing."

"Don't call the police on the Shepherds," Dani clarified. "Call them on yourself. You're trespassing in Omega City. Get arrested. You'll be safe in jail."

We all stared at her. I think my mouth was open.

"You're . . . really twisted, did you know that?" Mom whispered.

Dani didn't even flinch. "Can't help it. It's how I was raised. Now, will you help me?"

FIFTEEN MINUTES LATER, we were all standing at the launch terminal of another missile silo, staring into the hollow cylinder at the gleaming white sides of another rocket ship. This one was marked on its side with the name *Wisdom*.

Eric seemed skeptical. "For a man who left the Shepherds because he thought we should all stay on Earth, Dr. Underberg really likes his rocket ships."

"Duh. He was a rocket scientist," I said. "Besides, that's not why he left the Shepherds. He was just really sick of them lying to get their way." I glared at Dani, but she ignored me, as she was busy hacking into the computers there and readying *Wisdom* for takeoff.

Mom put her hand up against the glass and leaned forward, looking down into the depths of the silo below. "I'm still not sure how this glass is supposed to keep us safe."

"It's not," explained Howard. He pointed to the edges. "Before the missile takes off, there are multiple layers of blast doors and ceramic shielding that cover us and protect us from the rockets."

"Still," said Mom, her brow furrowed.

Dani wore a similarly uncertain expression, but I don't think it was because she was nervous about the safety of the launch station. After all, that would require her to actually care about us. No, she was busy working on the actual launch and flight plan, as well as making sure *Wisdom* was capable of life support and other mechanisms.

"You know what I don't get?" Savannah asked. "Why the Shepherds never found this place before we did."

Dani sighed. "They thought it was destroyed, and Dr. Underberg with it. Fiona was the only one who suspected the truth. But Guidant has all the money in the world to fix things up now, so as soon as we were made aware that it was here, we stepped in."

All the money in the world, I thought, as long as their secrets and lies stayed buried.

Howard was still admiring the ship. "So the Shepherds rebuilt it, just like the rest of Omega City?"

"Yes." Dani typed on.

"Why did they do that, if they had their own spaceships?" he asked.

"Howard, dear," said my mother. "Maybe don't bother Dani while she's, um . . . hacking?"

"It's okay," said Dani, not looking up from the screen. "They originally rebuilt the ship because they were trying to launch it to intercept Underberg's ship, *Knowledge*. The ships are twins, and have built-in flight plans meant to allow them to automatically join and link up once in orbit."

That made sense. If the people on the ships were all from Omega City, it only stood to reason that they'd want to find each other in outer space. "So you guys rebuilt it hoping that would be an easy way for you to find Dr. Underberg?"

"Exactly." The tapping of the keys became more furious.

Savannah made a face. "So why didn't you do it? I mean, wouldn't catching Dr. Underberg have been so much easier than kidnapping all of us and planting us on your space station as a trap?"

"They tried. Unfortunately, they never could figure out how to disarm the kill switch that kept the rocket from launching."

"What's a kill switch?" Savannah asked, her eyes wide.

"It's an automatic shutoff," said Eric. "You know, like the one in that elevator that almost gassed us when it thought we were Russians?"

"Oh," said Savannah. "Yeah. That's just like Dr. Underberg to put something like that on his rocket ships, to keep outsiders like the Shepherds from using it."

Dani pressed one more button, then sat back in her chair, a satisfied smile playing across her face as the lights on the launch terminal came alive. "But I just fixed it."

Above our heads, a dozen screens flickered to life,

showing the silo and the rocket from different angles. There were also views of what must be the interior of the space-ship. It looked a lot like I remembered *Knowledge*, with the big chairs for the astronauts and small rooms connected by round hatches and covered with storage and control panels.

"Wow," said Howard. "Are you sure I can't go inside? Just to see?"

Mom shook her head. "Who do you think you're kidding?"

Savannah leaned forward. "Wait, you fixed it? Just now?"

"Yep." Dani brushed her aside to set up the launch sequence.

"But aren't Guidant people all excellent computer programmers? You said earlier that the computers in Omega City were so ancient that a five-year-old with a cell phone could break in. So why couldn't they?"

"Maybe it's the same reason no one found Omega City before we did," I suggested. "Dr. Underberg hides things so only people who are his friends can find them. I'm sure it was something personal, right, Dani?"

"Uh-huh." She nodded, typing. "What Gillian said. Personal."

"So what was the code this time?" Savannah asked. "More Pluto stuff? Another number code?"

"Okay," conceded Dani. "Maybe not *exactly* the same."

"Do you ever stop lying?" Mom sounded exasperated.

And so did Dani. She groaned in frustration. "It was me, okay? I hacked the hackers. I didn't want them catching Underberg, so I made sure they couldn't disarm the switch and launch the ship. And now, I've undone my beautiful work."

"So *you* can catch him," I said, studying her. Mom was right. She lied about everything. She lied so much, maybe she didn't even know what the truth was.

"Yes."

Actually, she told me she didn't believe in the truth, just whatever story worked best for her. Which meant I'd better make sure her story was set before she left.

"And rescue my father," I prompted. "And Nate."

"Yes!" She threw her hands in the air. "Do we have to keep going over this?"

"Not if you don't keep changing your story."

She rolled her eyes. "I think that's my cue to blast off."

Howard came forward again. "Are you going to get in a space suit?"

Dani shook her head as she unzipped the hood of her utility suit. "These suits are positive pressure suits. All I need to do is hook them up to the machines inside and it should be sufficient for my flight. This isn't the moon mission, guys. Our technology is way better. I will, of course, be wearing a helmet. But those are inside the rocket, too."

Mom sat down at the launch chair Dani had vacated. "And it's all automated? To . . . blast you off and fly you to the other spaceship and everything?"

"Should be," said Dani as she tucked her hair inside her hood.

"And the blast doors and stuff? That's automatic, too?" Eric added. "I don't want to be fried."

"Yes, yes, yes."

I couldn't believe how casual she was acting about going to outer space. Then again, she said she'd done it before. I wondered if that was what happened when you were raised as a Shepherd—you came to believe that spaceflight was no more special than an afternoon drive.

She turned to my mother. "You'll call the cops when I'm gone, right?"

I guess that was another thing Shepherds were used to saying.

"Yes. I hope they can get in here without your voodoo." Mom gestured to Dani's box.

"Of course," said Dani. "I've disarmed the entry system. Anyone can come in now. I had to make it look like you all really broke in. And don't worry. I'm sure the police will believe you. After all, this isn't the first time the kids have trespassed in Omega City." She took one last check of her programming. "Well, this is it. Any messages for your father? Or Nate? Or Dr. Underberg?"

"Stay safe?" suggested Mom.

"Come home?" suggested Savannah.

"Remember everything you can. I can't believe you get to go into outer space!" whined Howard.

I looked at Eric. Eric looked at me. I couldn't think of any messages I'd trust Dani to deliver.

"Stay safe," I echoed at last.

"Yeah," agreed Eric. "And come home."

"And—" we both said at once, then stopped, gesturing at each other to finish.

"And we love you," I said.

Dani nodded. "Okay." Then she left the room. A few minutes later, we saw her silver-encased figure cross the walkway to the rocket, far below. A few moments after that, her frame came into view on several of the interior monitors. She was aboard *Wisdom*. We watched as she busied herself getting settled in the cabin, making sure everything was operational and online, and going through her final launch checks.

Eric sidled up to me. "Is this really going to work?"

I shrugged. I had no idea. "We've gotten this far."

"Yeah," he said. "And we've messed up every time."

"Not *every* time." I had to cling to something. "We got into Omega City okay."

"Sure," he said. "But do you think we're going to get out okay?"

I folded my hands in front of me, ignoring the sour pit of dread in my stomach. All this work to get out of Eureka Cove, and we were still in Shepherd territory. I watched Dani on the monitors. She was our last chance to save my father, and I barely trusted her.

Eric nudged my shoulder. "The good news is, we managed it last time, right?"

"Right," I mumbled.

He looked at Mom. "You know, I don't think you actually need to call the cops. They came the last time when the rocket took off."

Mom clasped her hands in front of her, squeezing tight. It made her seem nervous and small. I glanced down at my own interlocking fingers, and quickly released them. Oops.

"So we just wait, then?" Mom asked.

"Or we go," said Savannah. "Like, now."

"No!" cried Howard. "I want to see the rocket launch."

"Well, I want to not get caught by the Shepherds," said Savannah. "So which is more important?"

And then a loud, booming voice sounded through the room. A voice I knew well. Dr. Underberg and his recorded messages for Omega City residents.

Launch sequence activated—Rocketship
Wisdom.

Please evacuate all personnel and equipment from launch silo.

"Here we go!" Howard bounced again. He ran toward the window but, as promised, large plates of steel began to fold up and cover the view.

Mom watched the shields slide into place, but still looked concerned. "Do you think we'd be safer waiting elsewhere?"

Launch sequence paused. Deploy hex key to continue.

On-screen, we saw Dani pause whatever she was doing and look up, her helmeted face impossible to read. She quirked her head to the side as Dr. Underberg's voice repeated the instruction, then turned her attention to the terminal before her and started pressing buttons.

"What's a hex key?" Savannah asked.

"It's probably a hexadecimal code," Howard said. "It's a type of computer code. Base sixteen."

More codes. Well, at least Dani was well equipped to handle that. I watched her on the TV screen for a few minutes more. Her work was steady, unhurried and deliberate as the seconds ticked by.

I really hoped she knew what she was doing.

SECURITY

EXCEPT FIFTEEN MORE MINUTES PASSED, AND NOTHING CHANGED. DANI still worked furiously at the terminal near the pilot's chair, and the loudspeaker still repeated Dr. Underberg's messages of delay. After a while, he sounded a little peevish, though I'm sure that was just my imagination.

Launch sequence paused. Deploy hex key to continue.

"Is there a way to turn him off?" I asked at last. "It can't be good for her concentration."

"I'll help her," said Howard. "I'm good with codes."

"You'll do nothing of the sort," said Mom. She had turned on yet more screens in the launch terminal, showing exterior security footage of Omega City and the field above it. She kept nervously scanning them for signs of new arrivals. "We're all staying together, and far away from that rocket." She leaned in to look at one of the screens. "Oh, no."

There were cars pulling up outside the building where we'd entered. I saw dust clouding around the parking lot, and through it the shadow of dark sedans. Because of the camera placement, we had a bird's-eye view.

"Are they Shepherds?" Eric asked. I swallowed, my throat dry.

"Look." Howard pointed at one of the cars on the screen. You could just make out the glint of a light array on the car hoods, but no lights were flashing. "I think they are police."

"That's good news," said Eric. He looked confused. "Right?"

Mom squinted at the images. "But if they came to investigate, why aren't their lights flashing?" She looked at me. "Gillian, do you think they're really the police?"

I came closer. "I don't know . . . why are you asking?"

"Because your father isn't here, and I trust your opinion."

Her words hit hard and I blinked in surprise. Mom trusted my opinion about the bad guys—about *Them*.

Because like it or not, this was all very real.

On-screen, they opened the exterior door and came inside the building. I lifted my eyes to the next screen, the one displaying the entrance chamber and the elevator. Here, the picture was better, but as they rushed in, I still couldn't get a good enough view to make out a badge or anything. Dark clothes, thick belts—whoever these guys were, they were armed.

"I don't know. They might be?" But the Shepherds wore dark clothes, too.

"If they are the police, we can turn ourselves in. If not . . . we should hide." Mom bit her lip.

"What about Dani?" asked Savannah.

"What about the spaceship?" asked Howard. "She has to take off before the police get here."

I squeezed my hands together. If Dani didn't go, this had all been for nothing.

Mom nodded and turned to the communications array at the terminal. She flicked a switch. "Dani, someone has arrived here. It might be the police, it might be the Shepherds. Any advice?"

On-screen, Dani looked up, directly into the monitor, though her face wasn't visible behind the mask of her helmet. "Um, I'm a little busy at the moment. Trying to get to outer space, remember?"

"Is there anything we can do to help?" Howard blurted out.

"No." Dani went back to work. Her answer was clear—she had no advice for us. We were on our own.

Another ten minutes passed as we watched the intruders make their way through Omega City. I kept looking for badges or some other mark of their true identity, but when I thought about it, I realized it didn't make any difference. If the Shepherds wanted to dress up like police, it would be easy. Easier even than copying our voices.

"We should find a hiding place," I said, not liking the quake in my voice. "Just in case." Behind me, Savannah sprang out of her seat and started checking the closets.

On-screen, Dani took her helmet off and addressed us again. "Dr. Seagret, can you enter a code for me from your side?"

"Um, we're in the middle of . . . ," Mom began fretfully. "It's just that the kids . . ."

She exchanged quick glances with me.

"Mom, we have to help her take off. We have to. We'll go hide, but if she doesn't get up there, Dad—" I couldn't even say it.

Mom gave a short, decisive nod. "Right. Go. Hide. I love you." She turned back to the microphone. "Give me the code."

"Gillian!" Savannah beckoned me over to a set of cabinets. We wriggled inside, Howard and Savannah in one, Eric and me in the other. It was difficult shutting the doors from the inside, but we eventually managed. I found that if I angled my eye just right, I could see a slice of the room through the space where the door of the cabinet met the frame. It was just enough of a view to see my mother and three of the monitors. One still showed Dani at the spaceship. Another a shot of the walkway bridging out over the silo. And a third an empty corridor, somewhere in Omega City.

Launch sequence paused. Deploy hex key to continue.

We should have turned that announcement off. Where else might it be broadcasting in Omega City? If the new-comers heard it, they'd know exactly where we were.

We sat in silence as Mom and Dani worked. "Mom?" I said, after a minute or two. "Is there a lock or anything? A way to bar the door?"

"Dani, I'll be right back," Mom said over the loud-speaker. That may have been her doom, because just as she stood up, I saw figures on the walkway to the spaceship.

My heart stopped. *They were here!*

Eric found my hand in the darkness and squeezed,

hard. A sob caught in my throat.

On-screen, figures burst in on Dani. I don't know what I was expecting—her to fight them off, maybe? But she didn't. In a moment, she was subdued and they were leading her back across the walkway.

Mom stood frozen in the middle of the floor. "Don't make a noise," she whispered. "Listen to me. Don't make a sound."

The door burst open. Eric and I clung tightly to each other. I couldn't breathe. I couldn't think.

Figures in black surrounded my mother. I shied away from the crack in the door out of instinct.

They were all shouting at once, but I could barely take anything in.

Get away from the keyboard! Put up your hands! Do you have her? Don't let her get away. What are you doing here? What's your name? Where's your ID? Where's the other one? Who else is here?

"Don't talk to them, Grace." Dani's voice cut through the commotion. "Not a word."

I held my breath and leaned forward to peek through the crack again. Dani in her silver suit was kneeling on the floor next to my mother. They both had their hands fastened behind their backs.

"Where are the children?" asked a voice.

"What children?" Dani asked. There was a thump

and she sprawled forward, unable to catch herself because of the zip ties around her wrists.

"Dr. Seagret, where are your children?"

My mother's mouth remained shut.

"Do you realize people are looking for them?" the voice went on. "Don't you want them to be safe?"

Don't fall for it, I silently begged my mother. I knew this line of questioning. The Shepherds made it sound like they were on your side. But *they* were the ones looking for us. And she was the only one who knew where we were.

"Answer us now!"

On the floor, Dani was a flash of silver, and the room erupted in chaos.

Watch out! Quick! Stop her! What was that? What did she hit her with?

My mother slumped to the ground, her dark hair spilling over the floor. Beside me, Eric jerked, and I grabbed him before he could make a sound. But things were too crazy outside for anyone to hear us.

Eric was panting in my ear, and I realized that I was holding my breath. Mom was on the ground, only a few feet away. And there wasn't a thing we could do that wouldn't end up with us the same way.

Don't make a noise. Listen to me. Don't make a sound. My mother's last words to us echoed in my head and I breathed out as slowly and silently as I could manage.

Outside, I heard a struggle, and Dani seemed to be dragged out of the way, over to the edge of the room. *Our* edge.

"What was that!" someone shouted. "What did you do to her?"

"Animal tranquilizers," Dani replied calmly. "Though you're the ones acting like animals."

"Dr. Seagret. Dr. Seagret. Where are your children?" One of the guards knelt over her. "Hurry, hurry, she's losing consciousness."

"We hid them." My mother's voice was slurred and slow. "Somewhere safe." The man waited, but my mother didn't say anything after that. I'd forgotten how to breathe. Dani had lied again, broken her promise to my mother about using tranquilizers—and possibly saved us all.

"Where are they?" He barreled down on Dani, who was now quite close to my cabinet. I could hear the anger in his voice vibrating through the metal.

"Far away from here," Dani said. "Are you kidding? That woman was so worried about her precious tots, she refused to do anything to help me until we dropped them off with a friend of hers. You know the Seagrets and their links to the conspiracy community. They're probably way off grid by now."

I was impressed by that story. I guess if you had as much practice lying as Dani, it came easy.

"What were you thinking, Alcestis? Do you have any idea what you're risking?"

"Yes," she replied. "I know it perfectly. And I'd rather risk it than risk my father's life. You can tell Elana that, or I'll be happy to tell her myself."

"We'll see about that."

Just then, her eyes focused on me through the crack in the cabinet doors. "Yes, we'll see what happens now. You may have caught us, but it's not over. We'll be okay. And I've launched more plans than you can possibly imagine." Her gaze bored into mine.

"Ugh, shut her up, would you?" Someone dragged Dani away. Dr. Underberg's voice flowed through the room again.

Launch sequence paused. Deploy hex key to continue.

"And shut this down, too, while you're at it. The last thing we need right now is any unscheduled launches."

"Yes, sir."

"I've got to call for backup and find out where the children went. Dani has to have left some clue behind. We almost got it out of the mother."

They thought we really had been dropped off

somewhere, like the police station or Howard's house. Dani had been right.

Outside, the dark-clothed people continued bustling around, but it got quieter and quieter. My legs started to ache, but I was too terrified to move, afraid I'd make a sound. Eric and I clutched at each other for reassurance. More time passed. I have no idea how much. Months, probably.

Eventually, I was pretty sure we were alone, but I was still too scared to open the door and see. Eric and I looked at each other. I shook my head at the question in his eyes.

I heard a thump from the other cabinet.

"Ow, Howard, stop." Savannah. "I can't move any faster. My leg's asleep."

"Well, scoot over. I need to go to the bathroom *now*."

The silver of Howard's utility suit passed before the door. Eric and I leaped into action, scrambling out.

"Howard, wait! Don't leave the room," I hissed at him, but he was already halfway out the door. What if the Shepherds were waiting just outside?

"Ow ow ow," said Eric, hopping up and down on one foot. "Pins and needles, pins and needles."

Savannah and I hurried to each other.

"Gillian, I'm so sorry," she said. "I'm so sorry about your mom."

"Yeah." I felt numb about it, really. "But I'm still proud

of her. She didn't give us up, even as she was losing consciousness."

"That was awesome!" Eric agreed. "I had no idea Mom was such a good liar."

Neither had I. All this time, when the divorce was happening and we were selling our house and our boat and all this other stuff, Mom was the *good* one. The one who was following the rules. The one who had her career in shape and her priorities in place. She was the one who sent money and reminders to buy school uniforms, the one who rolled her eyes when Dad burned our dinners or lost our life savings or went on hour-long rants about government secrets and shadowy plots.

And now, she was the one who had lied to those same secret keepers—while being tranquilized—and saved all our butts.

Only, now what? We were alone, again, in Omega City. And no better off than we'd been yesterday.

"What do we do?" Savannah asked. "Do we call the cops now? The real cops?"

I puzzled over Dani's last words, which I knew had been meant for me. *You may have caught us, but it's not over. We'll be okay.*

"I think—I think Dani saw me in the cabinet. She doesn't want us to do anything about her and Mom."

Eric's jaw was set, but he didn't argue that point. He'd

heard her, too. "Mom's not going to be happy when she wakes up and realizes Dani knocked her out."

"Maybe." Or maybe Dani saved her life doing it. The Shepherds would have to wait until my mother woke up to ask where we'd gone. It might give us enough time to get away. But to where?

I've launched more plans than you can possibly imagine. She couldn't mean . . . us. I felt shaky.

Howard came back in, still zipping up his utility suit. "I'm back. But you guys all better go, too. It's way easier to pee down here on Earth than it is in space. Trust me on that one."

"What?" Savannah's eyebrows went into her hairline. "We're not going to space."

Howard looked at her like she was speaking gibberish. "Of course we are. Someone has to go get my brother and it's not going to be Dani now. So it has to be us." The words fell like tiny bombs into the landscape of my fear. Of course it had to be us.

I stared at him, in awe at his single-minded confidence as he crossed to the control panel and started turning things back on.

"Um, no it doesn't," Savannah said. "I'm *not* going into space."

The screens all flipped on, showing empty corridors, empty silos, empty cockpits.

"Howard!" Eric cried. "What do we say about pushing buttons?"

"Relax," said Howard. "I paid attention to what Dani did. Plus, the Shepherds left her little gray box. Look." He pointed, and sure enough, her little hacker box still stuck out of the port of one of the terminals.

"That doesn't make you Dani," Savannah said. "Or, you know, able to launch a rocket."

"You heard her!" Howard cried. "They are basically set to autopilot."

"Are you kidding?" Savannah shook her head in disbelief. "It's. Outer. Space."

Somehow, I don't think that warning had the effect Savannah intended, as Howard just grinned and went back to work.

"Gillian!" cried Savannah, turning to me in exasperation. "Say something."

Howard didn't even spare me a glance. I opened my mouth, but nothing came out.

Because Howard was right. Nate needed to come home. Dad needed to come home. And there was no one left to go get them but . . . us.

Still. Outer space?

"Gills?" Eric said, his tone fearful. "Gills?"

"We can't leave them up there," I whispered to Eric.

"We can't go get them, either."

"What's your suggestion, then?"

Eric ran a hand over his face. "We're not astronauts, Gillian. We're not. It was impossible when Dr. Underberg invited us to come with him last year. It's impossible now."

"Except Dr. Underberg is fine," Howard pointed out. "He went up into space ten months ago, and he's still there now. *Knowledge* was in a lot worse shape than *Wisdom* here is. And Dr. Underberg wasn't in as good shape as we are."

"*We*," said Savannah, "are kids. Astronauts need to do months of training. They need to learn how to do everything in zero g."

"That's why I suggested you pee before we leave."

"Sure. *Peeing* is the problem."

"It is. Astronauts have to train to do it."

She threw up her hands in frustration. "It's like talking to a wall."

"Gills," Eric added, gesturing helplessly toward Howard. "Do something."

I looked at Savannah. I looked at Eric. I took a deep breath.

Then I joined Howard at the keyboard. "How can I help us get to outer space?"

TURNKEY

ERIC GROANED. "WHAT? GILLS, NO."

"Gillian—" Savannah's words came at me as if from a great distance. I didn't answer. I didn't care. I was going to space, and I was bringing my father home.

Howard flipped another switch, and the voice of Dr. Underberg sprang to life once more.

Launch sequence paused. Deploy hex key to continue.

"You have got to be kidding me!" Eric cried.

"Okay," I said to Howard. "Now what?" This was as

far as Dani had gotten, and it still wasn't blasting anyone into space.

"Now go to the bathroom. Get ready. I'll go see what's going on inside the rocket."

There was a restroom conveniently located outside the launch terminal station. I used it, and while I was washing my hands, I looked at my reflection in the mirror. My ponytail was a mess; my utility suit looked rumpled. I smoothed out my hair. Were ponytails annoying in zero g? Maybe I should put it in a braid. A bun wouldn't fit under my helmet. A braid, at least, I could tuck down the back of my suit.

Sure, Gillian. Think of your hair when you're about to launch into outer space.

I was almost done braiding when I caught sight of Eric standing behind me.

"Do you know what Savannah and I have spent the last ten minutes doing?"

"No."

"Checking to see if Dani left any more tranquilizers behind. Gills. We can't talk Howard out of this. I know that. But I can't let you go. It's too dangerous."

I wound a rubber band around the end of my braid. "Everything we've ever done in Omega City has been dangerous. It was dangerous for us to scuba dive through a parking lot. It was dangerous for us to use grappling hooks to escape an exploding rocket ship."

"Yeah," Eric agreed, "but we didn't have a choice there."

I turned around to face him. "I don't have a choice, either. Someone has to get Dad. Someone has to get Nate. I'll be fine."

"Dad would not want you to risk your life for him." Eric grabbed my shoulders. "Astronauts die, Gills. They die all the time."

A shudder passed through me as I met his eyes. The usual teasing light was nowhere to be found. He was totally serious, and seriously terrified.

And so was I.

"Well, I'm going to make sure we don't. All of us." I slid my arms around his back and hugged him, hard. "I love you, Eric. Give my love to Mom and Paper Clip."

Then I pushed past him and back into the stairwell, but instead of going up, I went down. I don't know if he followed me. I couldn't bring myself to stop and check.

The door to the walkway opened at my approach.

Greetings, space explorers. You have arrived at the doorway of the Rocketship *Wisdom*. Please come prepared with your blood type, life-support gear, and thirst for adventure.

I took a deep breath and stepped out. This walkway was sturdy and solid, unlike the one I'd crossed the last time I'd gotten on a rocket ship in Omega City. I tried not to look down as I walked out above the void. Though since I was about to get farther away from the ground than most humans, the idea of being scared of this height seemed a bit silly.

The door lay open. Inside, it looked like a spruced-up version of Underberg's other ship. The same panels and screens and storage covered every inch of the interior chambers—but everything gleamed and shone in this one. I made my way down through the circular hatches connecting floor to ceiling into the pilot's chamber. Howard was kneeling by one of the chairs and checking a bunch of wires and tubes that protruded from its base.

"The life-support stuff seems to be in great shape," he said. "And they have all kinds of instruction checklists everywhere. I don't know what Savannah and Eric are worried about. A child could do this."

We are children, I thought. *And just because we can follow instructions doesn't mean we can launch a rocket.*

I looked at the screen showing the launch terminal. Eric and Savannah sat in the seats up there, their eyes glued to their own monitors. I waved, and watched their reaction.

I came closer and flicked on the audio. "Hi, Sav."

"Hi, Gillian." She didn't sound happy. On-screen, she folded her arms across her chest.

"Don't be mad at me!" I exclaimed. "You know I have to do this."

"I'm not mad," she said.

"I mean, don't worry."

"I'm not worried. Because you aren't going to do it."

"Yes, we are!" Howard shouted, then went back to work.

Launch sequence paused. Deploy hex key to continue.

Then again, maybe we wouldn't. "Um, Howard? Did you ever figure out what that code is that Dani was stuck on?"

"I'm doing that next." He held up some tubing. "Here, attach the life support on your suit."

You know what's a scary term? *Life support.*

Howard lifted the flaps of my utility suit to find the panel used to set the cooling or heating elements, then plugged two different wires and a tube into the ports there. The suit suddenly felt tightly squeezed around me and then, on a breath, puffed up until all the wrinkles stretched out.

"There you go. Pressurized. Want me to show you how to attach the helmet?"

I nodded and he got to work. The helmet was hard, with

an airtight seal around the base of my neck that tucked into the collar of my utility suit. My ears popped when he had it all worked out. I swallowed thickly and peered through the shadowy glass. All of a sudden, it seemed like too small a thing to really protect me.

And it was pointless, anyway, unless Howard unlocked Underberg's code.

"So, Howard?" I said, and my voice echoed around the inside of my helmet. "You do have the hex key, right?"

"I will."

Savannah was still sitting there smugly, watching us with crossed arms and a self-satisfied expression.

"Sav, seriously? I don't want this to be my last memory of you."

"Oh?" Eric snapped. "What happened to 'I'll be fine'?"

"It won't be your last memory," she said. "Because you aren't going anywhere."

Launch sequence paused. Deploy hex key to continue.

She grinned.

Inside my space suit, I stamped my foot. I could not believe she was *smiling* about all this. "Sav, this isn't funny. Dad's up there. Nate's up there. And no one can save them if we can't. Don't you get that? Nate saved *your* life last year. You almost drowned in that elevator"—I gestured vaguely to where I figured that chamber was in Omega City—"and he rescued you. We owe him the same thing."

The smile vanished from her face.

"Don't," Eric said to her as Savannah's arms dropped to her sides. "Sav, don't help them."

But Savannah had disappeared from view. Eric glared at me through the screen. I ignored him.

A few minutes later, she crawled down through the hatch.

"Savannah!" Howard exclaimed. He jumped out of his seat and started rigging up another one of the flight chairs. "Come try on a helmet."

"I'm not going anywhere," she said. She turned to me. "I'm here to help you take off. And I'm not doing it just because of Nate and the elevator, either. Besides, I already know you'll risk your life to save someone you love, Gillian. Because I almost drowned twice in Omega City, and it was *you* who saved me the other time."

My eyes began to burn and I took two steps forward and encased her in a hug. Even through the weird, rubberized sensation of my pressurized utility suit, I could imagine I felt her heart pounding as hard as my own.

She pulled away and wiped her eyes. "Now let's get you guys into outer space."

"How do you plan to do that?" I asked. "Suddenly learn codes?"

She shook her head. "You've got it all wrong. Dani did, too. The hex key isn't a code. It's an actual key." She held up the hexaflexagon zipper pull. "Now all we need to do is find the lock."

"How do you know this?" asked Howard. He crossed the chamber in a single step and went to snatch the hexaflexagon out of Savannah's grip, but she closed her fingers around it and held tight.

"It's the only thing that makes sense," she replied. "Dani said anyone could hack into the old computer tech on Omega City, but she couldn't figure out one measly hex code? And you said yourself that Dr. Underberg liked to make things easy for his friends to figure out here. What's easier than a key every single resident of Omega City would be wearing on their clothes?"

I looked at her in amazement. My best friend was a genius.

"You knew this whole time? Then why didn't you tell Dani?" I asked.

"I only figured it out when we were hiding," she said. "We were just sitting there, forever, so I started playing with the hexaflexagon again. And that stupid voice kept repeating 'hex key, hex key, hex key . . .'" She folded the hexaflexagon and revealed the bumpy side. In the light, I could see the pattern on the surface clearly—an arrangement of bumps and grooves and squiggles that covered every facet. "See?"

It did make sense to me. And it was just like Dr. Underberg, too. These rockets were for Omega City, and so he'd design it so that Omega City residents could use them. Maybe there were even directions on how, directions that had been burned up when I'd been forced to throw away all those instructional videos right before we escaped the last time we were here.

"So where does it go?" asked Howard. He pointed at the control panel. "I don't see any kind of hexagon-shaped lock anywhere here."

Savannah shrugged. "I don't know." She pointed at the pilot chairs. "Maybe there?"

I looked at the chairs again. There were six of them, arranged in three rows of pairs. Each was firmly bolted to the floor of the chamber, and covered with an oversized piece of fabric and a five-point seat-belt harness. When I touched the fabric, I felt the unmistakable squish of silicone gel inside. The side of my chair had printed instructions for activating something called *Shock Absorption Molding.* The instructions were marked with the Shepherd crest.

Shock absorption molding. I'd seen that before—in the pods Dani had used to transfer us out of the biostation! I thought back to meeting Dr. Underberg in his rocket, trying to remember what the pilot chairs had looked like on *Knowledge*. If these chairs were new, replaced by the Shepherds when they were refurbishing the rocket, then the hex key lock might be gone.

Launch sequence paused. Deploy hex key to continue.

I walked around the back of my chair, careful not to disturb the wires and tubes, but couldn't see anything.

A dead end. Again.

Howard was currently searching every button and switch on the terminal. I started scanning the walls, the storage lockers, the screens and readouts. Even Savannah was looking around, kneeling on the floor and running her hands over the tiles in case there was something useful there. But another five minutes passed with no progress. Dr. Underberg kept repeating his order, over and over, and I began to despair. We were never going to find it. We were never going to get out of here.

"You guys are idiots," said Eric, poking his head through the top of the hatch. He pulled himself in, dropped lightly to the floor, and picked the hexaflexagon up where Savannah had left it at the terminal. "It's a zipper pull on a jumpsuit. Where do you *think* the lock is? Not on the floor, I promise you that."

He came over to me and planted one hand on my shoulder.

"I can't believe I'm doing this." He tilted up the edge of my helmet and pressed the hexaflexagon onto a spot at the bottom of my chin. It clicked into place.

Instantly, a pale green light rimmed my visor shield and I heard a small metallic hum, like I'd put on a headset.

Hex key activated. Launch sequence in progress for Rocketship *Wisdom*.

INTO THE BLACK

THIS TIME UNDERBERG'S VOICE SOUNDED LIKE IT WAS COMING FROM inside my head.

"Eric!" I cried, and my voice echoed around in my head. "You did it! Thank you!"

"Cool!" Howard started fiddling with his hexaflexagon zipper pull until it, too, popped open. "Savannah, show me how you get to the key side."

While Savannah did that, I grabbed another helmet and turned it over in my hands. Sure enough, there, on the underside of the chin bar, was a small, hexagonal indentation. It even had the words *hex key* written above it.

Well, at least that explained why Dani hadn't found

it. She'd hacked the Shepherd system to keep them from disarming the fail-safe, but without being allowed into Omega City, she'd never seen these helmets firsthand.

Liftoff minus ten minutes. Please secure all persons and items for final launch status positions.

"I think that's our cue, Eric," said Savannah.

"Yeah," said Eric. He looked at Howard and me.

Howard, having attached his helmet and hex key, was now making sure his suit was wired into the system like mine. I knew he'd done it right when his helmet, too, lit up with a green line of light around the outside of his visor shield.

"Bye, guys!" Howard hopped into the front-most chair and started buckling himself in.

"Yeah," said Savannah. "Bye."

Both Eric and Savannah just stood there. I climbed into my chair and began attaching all the buckles. I was doing this. I was really going to go into space. I hoped I didn't throw up inside my helmet.

Liftoff minus nine minutes.
Rocket systems check. Life support check.

Navigational systems check. Silo surface release.

All systems go.

"The walkway is going to retract soon, guys," Howard said. "You'd better get a move on."

"Yeah," said Eric. "And the doors will seal. You know, trapping us inside."

"Then we wouldn't have a choice," Savannah said.

"Right," Eric agreed.

I whipped my head around and peered at them through the visor. "Are you guys for real?"

"No," said Eric. "I think we might actually be crazy." He pulled another helmet off the rack. "Because I can't make myself get off this ship."

Savannah sighed with relief. "Me neither. Someone pass me a hex key. I gave mine to Howard." She, too, grabbed a helmet.

I practically squealed. "You're coming! You're really coming!"

"Yeah," said Savannah. "I guess I have to."

I quickly disconnected my hex key and helped Savannah get into her helmet and wired her to her pilot chair. Howard did the same for Eric. By the time Dr. Underberg announced the three-minute warning we were all back in our seats.

Liftoff minus three minutes.

Retracting walkway. Sealing inner and outer doors of Rocketship *Wisdom*.

External rockets at 50 percent ignition status.

A loud roar began, very far away, and the rocket began to vibrate.

"Maybe we should inflate the shock absorption molding?" I suggested, reaching over to find the button on the side of my chair. My voice sounded tinny in my ears. When the others spoke, it was as if they were whispering from very near.

"Yes, great idea, Gillian!" Howard must have pressed his button, as ahead of me, his chair started to puff out. "Oh, this feels weird . . ."

I pressed the button. Just as in the transport pod, it immediately began to puff up around me and solidify, conforming to the shape of my legs, butt, back, and arms. Within a minute, I was half-encased in a giant molded seat that held me perfectly still. I couldn't even turn my head. Distantly, I heard the roar of the rocket's engines, and the rattling of the equipment, but the molding was shielding me like a cocoon.

Liftoff minus one minute. Switching to internal power.

"Oh no, oh no, oh no," Savannah was whispering under her breath.

"It's okay, Sav. Think about Nate," Eric said. Except I don't think Savannah's crush on Nate had survived throwing up on him the first time we were in Omega City.

"Sure," she replied, unenthused. "I'll think about how if I die trying to rescue him, he *really* owes me one."

Thirty seconds.

The roar became even louder. On-screen, the monitors showing scenes from inside the silo were replaced with a blinding white light. I didn't know if it was because the doors to the silo had opened or the rockets had caught fire.

I bit my lip. It was going to be okay. It was. *Dad, we're coming for you.*

> **Twelve.**
> **Eleven.**
> **Ten.**
> **Nine.**
> **Eight.**
> **Seven.**
> **Six.**

"Oh, you know what I forgot to do?" Eric said over the

sound of the countdown. "Go to the bathroom."

One.
Liftoff.

A sudden pressure glued me to my seat, like a giant invisible weight lay on me. But it wasn't nearly as strong as I expected, cocooned in my suit and the shock-absorption padding. I was expecting to be flattened. Instead, I just felt heavy, as if my suit were made of lead and held me down. There was a roar so loud even the noise-canceling effects of the helmet couldn't muffle it entirely. Ahead of me, the screens showed flashes of light and dark, rocket fire and night sky, but nothing that told me anything. We could be anywhere, or simply shaking and not lifting anywhere. I started feeling sick, then realized I was holding my breath. *Breathe, Gillian. Breathe.*

Then Howard's voice, calm and steady, broke through my fog.

"One minute into flight and we've broken the sound barrier. We're now moving faster than the speed of sound."

I tried to remember to breathe. I don't know what I expected from spaceflight. Something more intense, maybe? This felt halfway between a roller coaster and a bumpy plane flight.

"Now exiting the troposphere. Prepare for secondary booster rockets."

"How high are we?" Savannah asked Howard.

"Ten miles up," he replied. He sounded almost giddy.

Ten miles. *Up.* And moving faster than the speed of sound. I breathed in. I breathed out.

"Secondary rocket boosters will deploy in three, two . . . one."

A minor tremor, another jolt of acceleration. I fought against the pressure pinning me into my seat and clasped my hands in front of me. I thought about asking Howard how fast we were going now, but my mouth was dry and devoid of words.

The screens above our heads flashed with data, but none of it meant anything to me. There were tons of readings—maybe Howard understood them.

"Okay in there, Gills?" Eric said.

"Yeah. You?"

"Yeah. Mostly. We do know where we're going, right?"

I hoped so. I wondered what was happening to Mom and Dani right now. Surely the Shepherds knew the rocket had lifted off. Would we get them in even worse trouble?

"We're now moving at two thousand six hundred miles an hour and beginning to angle into place to increase to orbital velocity."

"What?" I blurted, my voice sounding shaky and strange in the headset.

"We've been flying straight up," Howard said. "Now

that we've exited the thick part of the atmosphere, the rocket will start moving at an angle and accelerating."

"Why?"

"Because if we don't, we'll crash back into the Earth."

I gripped my fingers tighter. What had we done?

"Two minutes and thirty seconds into flight," Howard said. He sounded so calm. I mean, he'd been planning for this his whole life, but still . . .

"Thirty-nine miles up and traveling at three thousand two hundred miles an hour," he reported now. "That would be fast enough to get us across the country in less than an hour."

Were we in space yet? How far up was space?

Another minute passed, and then another, in which the only sounds were the persistent roar of the engines and the rattles and beeps of the machines around us. Howard regularly updated us with flight information. Fifty miles up and five hundred miles away from the launch space. Sixty miles up and moving at four thousand miles an hour.

"Look how fast this fuel is burning," Howard said in awe. "Five hundred pounds a second. Wow, it's really hard to get people into space, isn't it?"

"How much do we have left?" I asked, worried.

"Um, like a third of a tank?" He leaned forward. "Four hundred thousand pounds."

"Oh, is that all?" said Eric, but no one laughed.

"How fast do we have to go?" Savannah asked.

"Seventeen thousand five hundred miles an hour," Howard said matter-of-factly. "We're only going six thousand right now."

I noticed that Eric didn't say *Oh, is that all* again. Would we even have enough fuel to make it? Everything started shaking harder than ever.

"Prepare to throttle down acceleration to preserve structural integrity."

I tried to lean forward but it was no use. "What? What did you just say about structural integrity?"

Howard didn't even hesitate. "At a certain point, we have to slow down the rate of our acceleration or we will break apart."

"Slow down? But I thought you said we needed to get to seventeen thousand miles an hour or we would crash!"

"Not slow down," said Savannah. "He's talking about acceleration. We'll just speed up a little less quickly than we've been speeding up so far."

That didn't make sense to me at all. Suddenly, I was breathing very, very fast.

"Gills? Gills?" Eric's voice cut through my panic. "Guys, I think Gillian passed out."

"No," I forced myself to say. "No, I'm okay." I closed my mouth and counted to five, then breathed out. My visor clouded for a second, then cleared. No one was talking.

149

The shaking had diminished. "I'm okay," I repeated.

Dad and Nate were lucky. They were unconscious through all this.

"So when do we become weightless?" Eric asked. "Because I feel heavier than ever right now."

"We have to get into outer space, silly," said Savannah. "We're still in the Earth's gravity."

"We'll always be in the Earth's gravity," said Howard. "The moon is in the Earth's gravity. People aren't weightless in space because of gravity. They are weightless because being in orbit is like being in a state of constant free-fall."

"No!" cried Savannah. "Wait, really?" She was quiet for a moment, thinking about this. "So the Earth still has gravity all the way up here?"

"Yes," said Howard. "That's what holds the moon in."

Leave it to Howard and Savannah to argue about physics while we were accelerating to ten thousand miles an hour. By the time they were done, my breathing was back to normal, and I'd gotten quite the lesson on how objects—like us, and Dr. Underberg, and Infinity Base—stayed in orbit. Apparently, once we were at the appropriate height and speed, the engines on the rocket would turn off, and we'd just . . . *fall*.

Except that we were falling so fast, and from so far up, that as we fell, the Earth would keep moving underneath us and we'd keep . . . missing the ground.

"Forever?" Eric asked in disbelief.

"No. I mean, there's some drag and friction and stuff. So occasionally we'll have to boost our speed or correct our course. It's kind of like how if you go to the top of a hill with your bike, you can coast all the way down, but eventually you'll start slowing, so occasionally you'll pump the pedals."

And it turned out that we weren't weightless in space. What we were was falling, constantly. Like we were stuck at the very top of a jump on a trampoline. A really, really, really high trampoline.

I'll be honest, a large part of me wished I'd studied as hard as Howard on space stuff. But I was relieved to have him here. Otherwise, we wouldn't have a clue what we were doing.

Ten minutes in, Howard announced that we'd achieved low Earth orbit, and the engines were shutting down. I couldn't believe it had only been ten minutes. It felt like years since I'd strapped myself in.

"Do you want to see it?" he asked.

"Yes!" we all cried.

He clicked a button and the overhead screens changed from data to a singular image—a great expanse of hazy blue, stretching all the way across the screen. At the top, the blue faded into an unrelenting black, and at the bottom, into a textured white, pockmarked by darker shadows that might have been the edges of a continent.

Again, I stopped breathing, and just stared. I think we all did. It was Earth, spread out below us. Massive, solid, blue and white. There was nothing around us. No identifiable shapes of the landmasses beneath us. Just one big ball and the unending blackness of space.

We were alone.

All I'd seen, all the wonders of Omega City and the horrors of Eureka Cove, paled in comparison to this. I was far from home, far from the reach of everyone I'd ever known or loved. I should have been terrified. But instead, I felt elated.

The scene on-screen seemed so real, like I could reach out and touch it, just poke that big blue ball slowly turning before us. Nothing could touch us up here. The Shepherds were insects, their plans and places and fears microscopic. The Earth wasn't going anywhere. Look at it! Humongous and bright, solid and whole.

"We did it." Howard broke the silence.

"We did it!" echoed Eric.

"We did it!" Savannah cried in agreement.

I still couldn't find words. My heart was full to bursting, staring at the vista of Earth and space. I don't care what Howard said—this wasn't falling. This was floating. Even strapped into my seat, I felt like I might drift away, like the walls of the rocket were nothing but paper and wishes, and might blow apart on a breath. But I'd remain.

"Earth to Gills . . ."

I heard him, but it took a moment for the words to sink in. "No," I said, barely able to contain my laughter. "*Not* Earth. You're nowhere near it."

Eric laughed, too. And then we were all laughing and cheering. We'd made it into outer space! Alone, strapped on the side of a rocket going, Howard announced proudly, fifty times the speed of sound.

"Can we take off our helmets?" Eric asked Howard.

"Let me check our cabin pressure." Howard looked down at the monitors on the display in front of him. "Yes, it looks like we can."

But before any of us had a chance to move, the lights and screens all flickered off. For a moment, we were in complete darkness. And when they came back on, every indicator light in the place was blinking orange. The screens above our heads lit up all at once, and I thought for a moment they were showing our own flight deck, with its rows of chairs and walls of machinery. But instead of four scared kids in utility suits, there was a lone figure—pale, emaciated, and seated in a central chair.

"Hail, *Wisdom*," said Dr. Underberg. "Please identify yourself."

BREAKAWAY

"DR. UNDERBERG!" I CRIED, STRUGGLING WITH THE FASTENERS ON MY helmet. "It's us."

"It's us!" added Howard. "Howard Noland."

"And Gillian Seagret!" I yanked the helmet up, where it wedged into the molded foam headrest around my chair. "And Eric and Savannah." I pointed out the others, who waved at the screen, though we weren't entirely sure where the cameras were. Or if they were on. Or if he could even hear us—as he said nothing in response, just sat there.

"Dr. Underberg?" I asked, confused. "Howard. Can he hear us?"

"I have no idea," said Howard. He pressed a button on

the array in front of his seat, but nothing happened to the screens. "I don't know what's going on. Nothing's working anymore."

"All functions of the Rocketship *Wisdom* are now under the control of the Rocketship *Knowledge*," Dr. Underberg said firmly. "And they will remain that way."

"Dr. Underberg?" I waved my hands in the air. "Can you hear us?" I figured he'd be happy to see us. Or something. But his expression was impossible to read.

"What's happening?" Savannah asked. "Is his ship coming for us? Are we going to him?"

"Dr. Underberg! We've come because the Shepherds have kidnapped my father—"

"Please refrain from broadcasting sensitive information during this transmission," Underberg stated. On-screen, his hands never stopped moving, traveling over the dials and keys and other controls in front of him. But he wasn't even looking while he worked, just staring straight into the camera. Straight at us. "Remain seated. Linkup will occur within the next one hundred minutes."

The large display switched back to the view of the outside.

I slumped—well, the little bit I could still manage to slump within the foam confines of my molded seat. I longed to be able to get up and stretch—or even shift position. My helmet, still partially stuck in the foam shape around my head, poked me in the back of my braid. I struggled to get enough leverage while still fastened in my seat to yank it out of the helmet-shaped cavity in the foam. I settled back into my seat and tried to put the helmet in my lap, but the second I let go, it began to float upward. Alarmed, I snatched it out of the air and hugged it to my stomach.

"Well, at least he knows we're here," said Savannah. "And he's coming for us."

I nodded, staring down at the helmet in my lap, but it was little comfort. In my mind, I'd figured that as soon as we got in touch with Dr. Underberg, he'd be able to help us. Everything we'd done since escaping Eureka Cove was to get to Underberg—the helicopter, Omega City, hiding from the Shepherds, *blasting off into space* . . . But he didn't even seem pleased to see us.

Then I lifted my eyes to the screen again, where the Earth lay spread out beneath us, white and blue and perfect, and everything else fell away. We were here. Dr. Underberg was coming for us. It would be all right.

After a few more minutes of just staring, Howard spoke up. "You know, everyone said we were supposed to feel sick. Do you feel sick?"

"No," said Savannah. "Why are we supposed to feel sick?"

"Because of the falling sensation. Because we don't know up from down. They call the plane astronauts use to train for weightlessness 'the Vomit Comet' because they get sick so much."

"Ew," said Savannah. But then she seemed to think it over. "Maybe we don't feel sick because we're strapped in. If we were floating around, maybe we'd feel it."

"That's probably why Dr. Underberg told us to stay seated," I said.

"I don't feel sick," Eric piped in. "And I don't have to go to the bathroom anymore, either."

"Eww! Eric!" Savannah pressed her hands against the side of her helmet, as if trying to cover her ears. "And you're *sitting* in it?"

"That's not what I meant!" Eric cried, embarrassed. "I just mean that it doesn't feel like I have to go anymore."

"Oh, that's because of the weightlessness, too," said Howard. "The sensation we're used to of needing to relieve yourself is because of the weight and pressure of urine in your bladder. Since we're weightless, our urine is, too. It will continue to fill your bladder until it explodes."

"*What?*"

"I told you to go before we left."

Eric turned to me. "There's got to be a bathroom on here, right? I don't want to explode."

"You're not going to explode," I said. Not in an hour or so, right? "Dr. Underberg told us to stay strapped in."

"Gills . . ."

"This is why astronauts wear diapers during takeoff and landing and any spacewalks," said Howard.

"I don't think I could do that," said Savannah. "Pee in a diaper? No way."

"You used to do it all the time when you were a baby," Howard pointed out.

"I'm not a baby," she snapped.

"But we're done with takeoff," said Eric, trying to steer us back to his own problem. "We're in orbit. We have to find a bathroom. Gills, there's got to be one . . ."

I sighed. "Howard, look at the diagram of the ship. Find the restrooms." I started to undo the clasps on my seat belt. Even after I was unbuckled from the straps, the molded foam of the seat kept me in place.

"The lavatory is in the next chamber down," Howard said. "It looks vacuum-based. Do you need instructions?"

"To go to the bathroom?" Savannah asked.

"To use the space toilet, yes."

Eric was busy untangling himself from his restraints. As I watched, he floated up out of his seat. I stared at him with my mouth open. Even though I was expecting it, it still looked like magic.

Except he kept floating up. And up. He tried to swim back down to the seat, but nothing happened. He started paddling furiously, and only turned upside down. "Hey!"

Savannah cracked up. "It's not water. You have to push off."

He rotated a little further around. "Push off . . . what?"

I chuckled. "I thought you were good at swimming, Eric."

He flailed even more. I shook my head. He was now . . . dangling? Was that what you called it in space? . . . about four feet above our heads, upside down and at a weird angle.

"Gills!"

"Okay." I pushed down, popping my legs and back-side out of the foam molding, but grabbed on to the seat before I, too, floated away. Slowly, deliberately, I allowed my legs to float above my head. This was a bit like scuba diving, when you had your buoyancy adjusted just right. Except unlike scuba diving, there was no way to swim through the air.

I kept my eyes on the seat, afraid of getting disoriented if I looked over at Savannah from upside down. That could happen when diving, too, especially if you were in the dark or in deep, deep water, where you lost track of which way was the surface. Except underwater, you could always follow the bubbles, which float up to the surface.

Here, there was no real up. And no real down, either.

"Grab my foot and come down here," I said. His hand locked around my ankle and I felt him climbing, hand over hand, over my utility suit. When he, too, had grabbed on to my seat with both hands, I risked looking over at him and rolled my eyes.

"Hey, remember when Dr. Underberg said we should stay seated?"

"Remember when I said you should go to the bathroom before we left?" Howard added.

"Remember when I said none of us should go to outer space?" Eric finished. "This isn't my fault. Now push me toward the bathroom."

"No more floating," I said. "We can climb."

And I did just that, grabbing on to the handholds in the side of the seat and on the floor. Angled as I was, it felt a bit more like walking my hands on an underwater pool ladder, or perhaps dangling from monkey bars. Hand over hand I went, toward the hatch in the floor.

"You look like you're both doing handstands," said Savannah. I turned to look behind me. Savannah had also removed her helmet, and the ends of her blond ponytail were fanning up around the back of her head like a peacock's tail.

We arrived at the hatch and I pressed the lever to open it. A loud pop and a whoosh of air startled me and I scooted back, afraid for a second that something was wrong with the air locks and we were about to be sucked out into space, but everything on the other side looked just fine.

"Um, Howard? It's all . . . life supportly in here, right?"
I asked him.

"Yes," he replied. "That pop was just a slight pressure differential. It should have evened out now.

"Hurry, Gills, before I explode," said Eric.

I pulled myself through the hatch and started making my way along the wall to the lavatory, but when I checked to see if Eric had followed, I saw him plant both hands on the wall on either side of him and shoot himself through the hatch and straight out into the middle of the room.

"Whoo!" he shouted, and rolled himself into a ball. As I watched, he somersaulted in midair and kept on going toward the other end of the chamber.

I hooked my foot around a railing and crossed my arms. Slowly, I floated around in a circle until I was upright. Or at least, until my head was toward the front of the rocket. "Oh yeah. Your bladder is *so* about to explode."

"Come on up here!" Eric said, kicking off the far wall and doing a loop-the-loop across the room. "Or down here. Or over here. Whatever."

"Tell me. Is this whole bathroom thing just an excuse to do weightless acrobatics?" I watched him land and push off again.

"Whee!" He cartwheeled past me. "No. I really do have to pee. Probably. But come on, Gills. When am I ever going to get another chance to do this?" He shrugged at me, upside down, then crashed into the far wall. "Ouch."

I slid my foot off the rail and kicked off the wall like it was the edge of a pool, gliding toward him. It didn't feel like swimming at all. There was zero control—I couldn't paddle or kick or change direction to stop myself, and though I put out my hands to catch myself on the wall, I came in faster than I liked, jamming both wrists as my body collided with the surface.

Howard poked his head through the hatch. "Getting your space legs?" He pushed out, too, floating into the middle of the chamber.

I rubbed my wrists, wincing. Maybe I should go back to wall crawling. It was growing a little crowded in here. Not only were there walls to crash into, now there was Howard's bicycling legs.

"Look, no hands!" Eric wafted by my head, his legs folded up on each other in lotus position, his hands upturned on his knees, thumbs and forefingers making twin Os. "I'm a master yogi."

"You're a loon." He smashed into the floor, headfirst. "Come on, let's get you to the bathroom."

Eric finally started working his way to the lavatory, while Howard tested out his newfound wings. I tried letting go of the handles set into the wall to see how fast I'd float. This was going to take some practice.

"Where's Savannah?" I asked Howard the next time he shot past me.

She called in from the other room. "We're passing through the nighttime now. It's amazing."

I abandoned my post at the wall and floated back toward the hatch. I wasn't halfway through the floor portal when I caught sight of the giant screen stretching from wall to wall above the command chairs and lost my grip. My body flowed through the portal and I rose up, past Savannah and above the chairs, until I was floating directly in front of the screen. It filled my entire field of vision, close enough to touch.

It was beautiful. Earth by night was a dark jewel, a deep, sapphire blue speckled and crisscrossed with spots and lines of sparkling gold that must be the lights of civilization. A halo of luminescent green surrounded the planet, like an iridescent bubble. I drifted, spellbound, as continents and oceans passed silently beneath my gaze, gilded coastlines and obsidian depths.

After some time, I became aware that Howard was beside me.

"It's spectacular," I whispered. "I can't stop staring at it. I feel like . . . I don't know, like it's mine, somehow."

"It is yours. It's all of ours."

"No. I mean . . ." But words failed me. Like it was *mine*. "Everything that I know has ever happened ever is down there. Hundreds of thousands of years of human history. Every second of all our lives. And it's all so small right now."

"Oh, yes," he said matter-of-factly. "That's called the breakaway effect. A feeling of euphoria, as if you are alone above the world. Very common in astronauts."

I frowned. This couldn't be common. No way. "You don't feel it?"

He considered this. "I think I always feel it. That's why I prefer outer space."

The world moved beneath us, at once utterly massive and impossibly small against the blackness beyond. Suddenly, the screen lit up with an arc of silver, a lovely crystalline cloud like the tail of a comet. It glittered across the screen for a moment and then was gone.

I gasped. "What was that? A meteor?"

Howard grinned. "Not exactly."

Far below us, Eric came back through the hatch. "That was even weirder than the toilets at Eureka Cove," he said. "It's kind of like peeing into a vacuum cleaner."

Horrified, I looked out at the view again, where I could just see the gross and gorgeous crystals floating away. "Oh, no. Don't tell me . . ."

"The Apollo astronauts said there was nothing more beautiful in space than the sight of a urine dump," said Howard.

So that fantastic sight . . . was my brother's pee. Gross. So much for the breakaway effect. Next he was probably going to tell me that green bubble surrounding the Earth was air pollution. I didn't want to hear it. It was all beautiful—the Earth and everything on it. Every last dirty, disgusting drop.

I stared down at our planet, our single precious planet, and thought about the lies that Guidant had been telling. How many astronomers were staring up at us right now and thinking they saw something else, because Guidant programs and computers were falsifying the records on their telescopes? And no one knew. Somewhere down there, Elana was probably staring up at us and planning her next move. If we could get to Dr. Underberg, we could help Dad and Nate, but what then? Elana still had Mom and Dani, and the Shepherds were lying to the world.

Eric floated up beside me. "At the risk of starting this entire process over again, did anyone think to pack anything to drink around here? I feel like I just ran a race."

"There should be provisions, yes." Howard floated back to the control panel to consult the diagram. "Ooh, there are actually snack packs built into each of our seats."

"Score!" Eric flipped over and started pulling himself back down to his seat.

Savannah craned her neck to look at us all. She alone remained strapped in, and her face seemed a little pale, the roots of her hair damp.

"Are you okay, Sav?" I asked, pulling myself down to her level. Upside down, I couldn't quite make out her expression, but it was proving harder to flip back around than I'd hoped.

"No," she grumbled, "and you guys acting like this place is your own personal circus tent isn't helping matters."

"Are you getting sick?" Howard volunteered. "Do you want me to find you some seasickness medicine?"

"Spacesickness," Eric corrected. He'd found an insulated packet Velcroed to the side of his seat marked *Food and Water*, and yanked it free.

"No!" Savannah turned away. "Just . . . stop talking about crystallized urine and . . . come sit down, okay? You're making me dizzy. Besides, Dr. Underberg said to stay seated."

There was the sound of crinkling and plastic packets being opened, and we turned to watch Eric scramble as handfuls of peanuts, chocolate candies, and raisins floated up into the air.

"Trail mix, on the loose!" he called, and started chasing them down, mouth open to catch all the flying food.

Despite herself, Savannah giggled. "He's impossible."

"Tell me about it." I crossed my arms and watched him Pac-Man around the cabin.

Savannah plucked a flying almond out of the air. "Over here, E." He wafted toward her and she flicked the nut into his mouth. "Score!"

I headed back to my seat. Ahead of me, Howard was sorting through his own food provisions. The water was contained in a soft-sided foil container, a bit like a juice box. The labels were all stamped with Shepherd markings, which, oddly enough, made me feel better about trying them. At least they weren't as old as Omega City. I reached down to detach my own package. I was a little thirsty, after all.

"Do you have to do anything special to the water?" I asked. "Could it float up and go up my nose?"

"There's a straw." Howard waved his own water container in the air. "Just drink regularly. But you could also do this."

He squeezed the container, and a big, bubbly ball of water appeared on the end of his straw. He gently shook it and it came loose, floating in the air. I looked closer. It wasn't a bubble at all, but a strange, clear, gelatinous ball of water. Howard leaned forward and ate it. Then coughed and sputtered.

"Okay, that was a bit harder than the astronauts make it look. Guess it takes practice."

I sucked on my straw for a minute. The water flowed up as usual, and into my mouth and down my throat, same as always. I took the straw away from my mouth and tried to squeeze out a bubble of water. The first one I tried was tiny, barely more than a droplet. When I clamped my lips down around it, it felt like nothing at all.

I tried again—a bigger squeeze, a bigger ball of water. I went in for the kill but missed completely as the ball floated above my mouth and splashed me right in the face.

Maybe I'd just stick to the straw.

The lights flickered off, then orange again, and I slammed into my seat. Eric dropped out of the sky on top of Savannah, who screamed. Howard was hanging on to the back of his chair for dear life. So much for free-fall.

"Eric!" I shouted. "Are you okay?"

"Urngggh," he moaned as he slid to the floor, clutching his head.

My stomach dropped into my toes. I tried to reach for the seat belt, but my arms felt as if they were moving through mud.

Dr. Underberg appeared on the screen in front of us. "Prepare for linkup," he said, then peered over at us, lying topsy-turvy all over the cabin. "I thought I told you to stay seated."

THE MAN IN THE HIGH SPACESHIP

HOWARD TURNED OUT TO BE MILDLY BRUISED, AND I HAD A SORE BACK-side, but it was my brother who ended up the most injured as a result of his fall. I helped him crawl back to his seat, despite the g-force hindering our movements. He had a nasty-looking gash above one eye, and was dragging his left leg. Of course, we were both dragging. Moving at all was like wading through peanut butter.

Savannah craned her neck to look back at us. "Is anything broken?"

"Is it broken?" Eric asked me.

I felt through his suit, but I had no idea how you could tell. There weren't any bones or anything sticking through.

Thank goodness for small favors.

"I'm not sure."

"Just once I'd like to get out of here with all my bones intact."

"Then maybe stay in your seat?" Savannah suggested. "Like you were told?" She turned back, but I heard her muttering under her breath. "Or, you know, not shoot ourselves into outer space. That might have been a good idea."

"Better get buckled in," Howard announced. "Looks like Dr. Underberg is accelerating us to a higher orbit."

"Is that why we aren't weightless anymore?" Savannah asked. She was already getting her helmet back on.

I turned to Eric, who was struggling to get his arm through his seat belt.

"You okay?"

"I'd better be," he said through gritted teeth.

"Gillian!" Howard shouted. "Back in your seat."

Eric snapped his belt closed, wincing a bit. "I'll be okay. Go get buckled in."

Slowly and treacherously, I pulled myself over to my seat. Every inch was a marathon, and I felt like I was moving my body through maple syrup. The machinery around us was vibrating again, hinges and drawer handles rattling. I clamped my jaw shut to keep my teeth from chattering as I hauled myself into the foam seat, arranged my legs and arms inside the depressions, and yanked my helmet back on. I grabbed for the seat belt and buckled my body in tight.

"Okay, Gillian?" Howard asked.

I swallowed. No. I'd been flying, and then I crashed. Hard. Eric looked like he might need stitches. I had no idea what was happening outside our little spacecraft, and Dr. Underberg didn't look like he was in the mood to explain. Above us, the screen showed flashes of undecipherable data.

"What's going on out there?" I asked instead.

"We're . . . going fast," Howard said. "Very fast."

"Why?" Savannah asked.

"I think so we can catch up with Dr. Underberg. I think."

Great, so Howard didn't know, either.

"Doing okay, Eric?" Savannah asked.

"Yeah," he mumbled. "I mean, blood is kind of dripping into my eye and I can't wipe it off because of the helmet . . . but I guess that's my fault for getting out of my seat."

"I hope you didn't break anything," Savannah said. "I remember how much that hurt when I broke my arm in Omega City."

"Yeah," said Howard. "But here he's weightless."

"What difference does that make?"

"He won't have to walk on it if it is broken."

"I didn't have to walk on my arm."

I sighed. The shaking and rattling—and bickering—went on for another half an hour, then began to smooth out. I stopped feeling like I was about to turn into a pancake.

"Are we there yet?" Eric asked.

"We're in a higher orbit," said Howard.

Dr. Underberg appeared on-screen again. "Hold for correction burn. Please stay seated this time." The screen switched back to data. I wondered if Dr. Underberg could hear us. If he even cared.

More acceleration, this time in short bursts. No one was talking much anymore. I began to feel tired. What time was it back home? How long had we been in space?

Should I have gone to the bathroom earlier, when I had the chance? I remembered what Howard said about not being able to tell when we had to go because of the weightlessness.

Just when I thought I couldn't take it anymore, the screen overhead switched again to an external view, and there, outlined by the blackness of the sky and lit by earth-shine, was the Rocketship *Knowledge*. Or what was left of it.

"Where's the rest?" I cried, horrified.

"Huh?" said Howard. "What do you mean? It's intact."

Barely! Even from this distance, I could see the scrapes in its paint across its surface, and there was also a large patch near the bottom that appeared to have been burned almost black. But that wasn't what concerned me.

"That can't be *Knowledge*. I saw it in the silo. It was a hundred feet high." The ship in front of me was . . . well, it looked like a candle left burning too long. Just a little stub.

"You're imagining the entire launch apparatus," Howard said. "We jettison several stages of the rocket during liftoff. Only the top part ends up in space. The rest of it is just for holding fuel to get us there. Think about the space shuttle. It's just strapped on the side of the big red rocket. We weren't strapped on the side; we were attached to the top. Be glad we aren't as small as the Mercury capsules were. They were just a tiny little nose—not even room to stand up."

"Did that happen to us, too?" I asked. "We're just a little . . . thing up here?"

"Yes," he said. "The rest of the rocket fell back to Earth. Probably in the ocean somewhere."

"Probably," scoffed Savannah. "Like the oceans don't have enough pollution without worrying about rocket fuel."

Knowledge drew slowly and almost imperceptibly closer. Minutes passed, or maybe hours. But nothing seemed to change. Dr. Underberg's ship moved, achingly slowly, off the screen entirely, leaving nothing but a field of stars. I realized that although we looked like we were just drifting in space, we must be moving at tremendous speeds in order to maintain this weightless feeling, and that Dr.

Underberg must be acting with extreme precision to bring our ships into alignment. I held my breath inside the suit.

"You still okay back there, Eric?" Savannah asked, as if I wasn't sitting next to my brother.

"He's fine, Sav. Stop freaking out."

"My leg is actually feeling better," Eric said. "Thank you for asking, Savannah. It's nice to know someone cares." He turned to me and glared.

"I care. I just have other things on my mind. Like how an old man is going to link two spaceships going seventeen thousand miles an hour."

Just then there was a metallic whirring from the chamber below us, and a few clanks that made my heart leap in my chest.

For a full minute, we didn't move, waiting for Dr. Underberg to appear on-screen again and tell us when it was okay to get out of our seats. But again, nothing happened.

"Howard?" I asked at last. "Do you see anything? Are we linked up?"

Howard studied the monitors. "It looks like we are. Our systems are still under the control of *Knowledge*—not just the propulsion system, but life support, communications, even the deployment of our solar arrays . . ." He pressed a button. "And the door is unsealed in the next chamber."

Savannah sat up. "So we should go?"

"I guess so."

She yanked off her helmet, unbuckled her belt, and gingerly slid out of her seat, making sure to keep a firm grip on the padding so she didn't fly away. "Good. Because I think I need to learn how to use that space toilet."

AFTER THE REST of us had gotten out of our seats and helmets and taken a turn at the lavatory, and I'd found a first-aid kit and cleaned and bandaged the wound above Eric's eye, we crowded around the hatch linking the two spaceships. It wasn't any larger than any of the other ports we'd been crawling through, but somehow, this one scared me more. Were the seals to be trusted? Was everything okay over there in *Knowledge*? Why hadn't Dr. Underberg contacted us with instructions?

Of course, even back in Omega City, he hadn't always made a lot of sense, and that was before he spent the better part of the year in outer space. Still, we'd put ourselves in his hands. Underberg was our last, best chance to get to my father and Nate. We had to do this.

Directions for opening the door were printed right there on the side. The locks and levers were even numbered, like you sometimes saw on airplane emergency exits.

Squaring my shoulders, I began the process. I held my breath as I released the latch, steeling myself for the possibility that I'd just opened the door into the vacuum of space, but there was a small, sucking pop, and the door revealed another chamber, just beyond the threshold.

I ducked my head and pushed myself through the portal. The others followed, Eric moving just fine without the stress of having to put weight on his injured leg.

Dr. Underberg's spaceship was like a mirror image of our own—or, more accurately, a set of before-and-after photos. Where *Wisdom* was bright and shiny, *Knowledge* was dented and scratched, its surfaces grimy, its air stale and acrid. It smelled like a dirty locker room. I reminded myself that *Wisdom* had been recently refurbished by the Shepherds, not to mention that you couldn't exactly let in fresh air on a spaceship.

"Hello?" I called. "Dr. Underberg?"

There was no answer. I drifted up through the empty, silent chambers toward the command module. *Déjà vu.* I'd taken this same trip before, back when gravity was an issue and this rocket stood in Omega City. Just like last year, I found him seated in his command chair, slumped and asleep at the controls.

"Dr. Underberg?" I said softly. "We're here. We're . . . docked or whatever."

He shook and looked at me, his eyes bleary. I bit my lip. The man I'd met in Omega City had been old, pale, sickly-looking. The first time I'd seen him, I thought he was dead. But that Dr. Underberg could have run a marathon compared to the person seated before me.

He was a skeleton. A skeleton covered in papery skin. There were sores on the backs of his hands, scabs on his nearly hairless scalp, crust around his ears and eyes and the corners of his mouth. Before I realized what I was doing, I shied away.

"Don't be afraid, Gillian," he croaked. "You've come all this way to see me."

I swallowed and looked back at the others, who were smartly keeping their distance near the floor of the chamber.

"Like Dorothy to Oz," he added dreamily.

Well, he was right that this wasn't Kansas, but other than that, I didn't feel much like Dorothy. And I didn't want to go home, either. Not until everyone was safe.

"Dr. Underberg, we need your help." Quickly, I explained what was going on with my father and Nate and the Shepherds.

"And from what Dani said, the idea would be to lure you back to Infinity Base to rescue them."

"Ah." He gave a creaky nod. "In that goal, they will fail. I cannot return to Infinity Base." He raised an emaciated hand. "I cannot even leave this chair. These months in microgravity have not been good to my old body. My muscles have degenerated; my bones have broken down. I am a china doll, Gillian Seagret, not a space ranger."

I shook my head. "But what do we do about Dad and Nate?"

He thought about this for a moment. "Well, *you* could rescue them."

"Why would it be any safer for us?"

"It would not be," said Underberg. "But they are not safe there, either. And if I brought you, I could complete my own mission of destroying the Shepherds' web of lies, which would also liberate your mother and Dani Alcestis."

"Your daughter."

The look he gave me was hard. "Perhaps."

I blinked in surprise. It was true they'd never met, but they'd been exchanging coded messages for months. If he didn't think she was his daughter, why did he trust her at all?

"Do you know what's happening on the base?"

"Yes. I've infiltrated their systems to give me regular reports, and that is something the Shepherds are aware of. I am always careful to keep my distance from Infinity Base when they have staff present. This will not be easy. But you are extraordinarily capable children. You have beaten the Shepherds at their own game. Stolen a spaceship out from under their very noses. I know they have been trying for months to take *Wisdom* from me, to use it to reach me."

"Dani kept them from doing that."

"Did she? Did she really? How clever of her."

He was quiet for a second, and I thought he might fall asleep again. What must it have been like all these months, alone in space? All those years, alone underground? He had no idea how to have a conversation.

His eyes opened again. "It's good that you have brought me a new ship. As you may have seen, this ship—and I— are both running out of time. I have managed for months to carry on by taking supplies from Infinity Base, but I have reached the end of that road as well."

Because he couldn't get up. I gritted my teeth, then dared to reach out to him. His skin felt like crumpled tissue paper beneath my fingers. I was scared to give him more than the briefest, featherlight touch. "Dr. Underberg, it's time to come home."

He stared at my hand on his, then lifted his gaze to my face. "So . . . you are Dorothy."

"No, I'm Gillian!" I didn't like this at all. He'd grown dreamy, forgetful up here. Or maybe he'd always been like that. It was possible I'd been hoping for too much from Dr. Underberg—I'd expected him to be some sort of wizard who could wave a wand and solve all our problems. But I still needed him to try. We didn't have magic slippers or good witches that could save us.

"We can go home," I promised. "But first we have to save my dad and Nate. How do we get to Infinity Base?"

Thankfully, he shook off his reverie and focused again. "It will take fourteen hours."

"Fourteen!" That was practically an entire day!

"It's very distant."

"But I thought when you orbit, you go around the Earth every hour and a half."

"Yes, but we cannot fly in a straight line to Infinity Base. We must slowly and carefully adjust the speed and trajectory of our orbit so as not to fall out or use too much energy as we match theirs." Dr. Underberg held up his hands, with two fingers making slightly different sized circles in the air. "Plus, we need to approach during their sleep schedule. Attempting to dock at the station while Shepherds are on board . . ." Dr. Underberg shook his head. "It may be impossible." He turned to his control panel. "And it may be playing right into their hands."

I frowned and looked back at the others, who were huddled around the hatch in the floor, watching with worried expressions. "So what do we do?"

"Now?" Dr. Underberg had already started plotting a course for the two ships. "I recommend you sleep. As much as you can. I have a feeling it has not been much the past few days. You will need your rest if you are to infiltrate Infinity Base." He waved me off.

"Do you need anything?" I asked. "Supplies from *Wisdom*? A . . . change of clothes?" My nose wrinkled of its own accord.

He cast me a sidelong glance. "I'm glad you have come, Gillian. Better late than never."

He meant because we didn't come with him, back when we were all in Omega City. The idea had sounded crazy then. Seeing what had become of him, it still seemed nuts. On the other hand, here I was anyway. Here we all were, and in more danger than ever.

I floated back to the others, who were more than happy to retreat into the cleaner, sweeter-smelling *Wisdom*. Howard practically hummed with excitement as he showed us how to ready the sleeping quarters, which were essentially thin, silky sleeping bags Velcroed vertically to the wall to keep us from floating away. We all had another snack, took one more trip to the bathroom, then zipped ourselves in. I looked around at the others, hanging up around the outside of the chamber.

"We look like cocoons," I said.

"Great," said Eric. "Now I'll never get to sleep."

"I don't know how I'll be able to sleep, either," said Savannah. "I'm in outer space."

"Right?" Howard agreed happily as he pulled his eye mask up on his forehead.

I thought about Dr. Underberg, trapped in his chair in the next room. He looked like he was dying. And if something happened to him, I put our chances at making it out of here at precisely zero.

Now I doubted I'd be able to sleep, either.

MISSION IMPOSSIBLE

I WAS WRONG ABOUT THAT. THOUGH IT TOOK FOREVER FOR MY BRAIN TO shut down that night, eventually, my body won. And here's the thing about space sleep—you've never been so comfortable. There's no need to toss and turn when every position is exactly the same. By the time I woke up, I'd lost all sense of up and down, night and day, time and space. I could have been sleeping for a few hours or a few millennia.

When my eyes opened again, Savannah and Eric were still out cold, their eye masks covering their eyes, their arms dangling out in front of them like cartoon sleepwalkers. Howard's sack was empty. I slipped out of my cocoon, rubbing my face. It felt full and puffy, and my nose was all stuffed up, like I had a cold coming on. I went to find Howard. The good thing about a spaceship was he couldn't have gone far.

As I suspected, he was in the *Knowledge* command center, chatting with Dr. Underberg. Well, Howard was chatting; Dr. Underberg was alternately staring at him and drifting off into little catnaps, which didn't seem to bother Howard at all. Or even stop him from talking.

He went on like this for a while, giving Dr. Underberg a moment-by-moment rundown of every step we took in Omega City to get onto the rocket, what happened during the liftoff, every stage of the launch . . .

A lot of it went over my head, to be honest. I was just glad it worked the way it was supposed to.

Still, I had questions, lots of them. "Dr. Underberg," I said. "Why did you send Howard that code book?"

"It's very important to know what the enemy is thinking."

That didn't make any sense. "It wasn't the enemy sending those messages, though. It was Dani."

His eyes slid in my direction. "And what did Dani's messages tell you?"

"What the Shepherds were thinking," blurted Howard.

"But—" My mouth clamped closed in frustration. Mom had been right. It was a game. A stupid game whose rules we didn't figure out until we'd already walked into the Shepherds' trap.

If he hadn't wanted to play these stupid games, would Dad and Nate be safe now?

Howard and Dr. Underberg went back to discussing the ins and outs of the spacecraft. It seemed as if Howard had been up early reading the manual or something, because he appeared to know every detail by heart. At least someone was having fun on this endless trip to Infinity Base.

Space was far too big. My nose was feeling more congested by the minute. I thought waking up and moving around would help, but maybe things worked differently in outer space. I tried to imagine a cough or a sneeze in microgravity—the danger of little balls of snot floating all over the inside of the ship.

I'd better find a tissue.

There were some in *Wisdom*'s bathroom, and I blew my nose, but it didn't do much good. I started to wonder if maybe I wasn't stuffed up after all. In the little mirror in the bathroom, my face looked fuller than usual, and I couldn't tell if it was a trick of the reflection, or possibly the result of the microgravity.

I was getting used to using the bathroom in space. The first few times I'd been scared I wouldn't position myself correctly over the seat, but now, the narrow opening and the suction almost seemed to work better than the regular toilets back home. At least you didn't have to worry about anything splashing you. It probably helped that I had a lot of practice camping, and figuring out how to go in the great outdoors. I wasn't freaked out by the fact that you weren't really sitting on anything.

After I washed up with antibacterial wipes and pinned the flyaways on my hair back, I returned to Dr. Underberg's command center, where Howard was still talking.

They seemed to be getting along pretty well, too, which made me wonder how Howard might have done if we'd let him go to space with Underberg last year, when he first wanted to. Then I got closer and caught sight of Underberg's skeletal frame, and remembered why that was a horrible idea.

This room, like the others, was grimy, surfaces sticky and covered with crumbs from meals he'd probably consumed months ago. It wasn't right that a man who had done so much for the world was stuck first under it and now above it, watching from afar.

Howard and Dr. Underberg were discussing the detailed points of some kind of complicated orbital maneuver that Dr. Underberg used to move the spaceships closer or farther away from each other without wasting precious fuel. It seemed he had very little left in *Knowledge*, and that most of the ship's life-support systems were running on solar power.

"Is it enough to land with?" Howard asked.

"Probably not," said Dr. Underberg. "But I don't believe I'll be returning to Earth."

My mouth opened with a squeak and they both turned to look at me.

"But Dr. Underberg," I said. "You have to go home eventually. Your daughter's there. Don't you want to meet her?"

Dr. Underberg lifted one delicate arm. "I don't think I'd last too long down there. And that's not even counting the fact that the Shepherds want me dead."

He said it so matter-of-factly, but I was horrified. I opened my mouth to argue, but he turned back to Howard.

"So what were the altitude parameters for the second-stage rockets? I fear they messed with my settings."

Okay. I knew when I'd been dismissed. Besides, who wanted to talk about dying in space? Not me. I went in search of food. This time, I was going to make sure he ate something from *Wisdom*. For all I knew, he'd been living on packets of Omega City astronaut ice cream all this time.

AS THE HOURS passed, we all became more adept at moving through zero g. Eric's twisted ankle healed nicely since he was able to stay off it to move around. I got dizzy a few times, and Savannah threw up once, but other than that, we were all tolerating space pretty well. For the time being.

Every time I caught sight of Dr. Underberg's withered limbs, I thought about the toll this life took. If this was what the part we could see looked like, what was happening with his internal organs?

At long last, he called us back into the command module. "We've arrived in the orbit of Infinity Base. Soon we'll be able to complete docking. Would you like to see it?"

I nodded furiously, and he switched on the overhead screen.

"Behold."

My brow furrowed as I took in the sight before me. I don't know what I was expecting from Infinity Base. The Death Star, maybe, or at least the Starship *Enterprise*. But the space station looked more like a wacky metallic flower. Several thick, bulbous cylinders formed the segmented stem. Each segment sprouted a pair of giant solar arrays, spreading from the center like massive, mirrored leaves. Other protrusions, like thorns on a rose, stuck out here and there from the stem. And then there was the "blossom" itself, a series of massive rings radiating out from one end of the station, each larger and wider than the last, forming a sort of cone. As I watched, I could see that the rings were slowly turning. In the center of the stacked ring cone were more structures, spherical dishes and more solar arrays, like the stamen of a flower.

"The entire base is modular," Dr. Underberg explained.

"They are constantly adding new parts, making it bigger."

Into infinity.

"That fourth ring is new." He pointed at the widest part of the blossom. "It's bigger than a football field. They're almost to half g."

"Half g?" I asked, confused.

"One g is the same gravity as Earth," said Howard.

"You're saying they have artificial gravity in there?"

"No," said Dr. Underberg. "It's centrifugal force. The rings rotate at a rate sufficient to create centrifugal force. It's like riding on a Tilt-A-Whirl or a merry-go-round—as the machine spins, you are pressed to the outside."

That made sense. "But how does that make gravity?"

"It creates the illusion of gravity. In the case of these rings, the floor is built toward the outside, with the inside of the ring as the ceiling of your design. You would essentially walk around on the outside without knowing it. The faster the rings spin, or the larger the radius, the stronger the centrifugal force. With careful design, you can simulate the effect of gravity within an extraterrestrial structure." He gave me a dirty look. "I had thought you'd read my research. This is all based on one of my designs."

Howard piped up. "Dani showed us your designs, as well as the updates the Shepherds made."

Dr. Underberg grunted.

"So each of these rings has a larger gravitational—I

mean, centrifugal force than the one before?" I asked.

"Yes."

Savannah tilted her head, watching the rings move. "Why don't they just move them faster?"

"Probably takes a lot of energy," Howard said.

"Oh, the problem is simpler than that," said Dr. Underberg. "If you spin too fast, the residents will get dizzy, for the same reasons you get dizzy on an amusement park ride."

Savannah appeared unconvinced. "But how do you make the force strong enough to be used like gravity but not strong enough to make you dizzy?"

I shook my head. I didn't understand any of this. "If spinning around makes everything fly to the outside, how come we felt gravity pulling us to the center of the Earth?"

"That's real gravity," Dr. Underberg said. "Like I said, centrifugal force is just . . . *faking* gravity."

"How does real gravity work?"

"Ah," said Underberg. "That's a mystery that better minds than mine have tried to unravel." He turned back to the image on-screen. "But what is important is fooling our brains and body into thinking that there is gravity. We've evolved to expect it. Without gravity, our sinuses clog up, our muscles deteriorate; all kinds of unfortunate things happen to our bodies."

That explained my stuffy nose.

"So if we want to live healthily for long lengths of time in space, in these bodies, and not end up like me, then we need to figure out a way to create a gravity-like force. And this is as close as any human has managed to get. So far. The ideal structure is probably over a thousand meters in diameter, spinning at a rate of once per minute to give you a nice, Earthlike feeling. But we're a long way from that."

I stared at Infinity Base. Were we? It was already closer to reality than almost any person on Earth knew. I looked at Dr. Underberg quizzically. He sounded almost . . . impressed by the Shepherds' accomplishments. But weren't they his enemy?

"We will be docking in a few moments. I've timed our approach during their sleep cycle, which should give us the best chance to sneak up on them. Their computer systems have been altered to conceal any records or notifications of my arrivals, and all indications show these hacks are still in place. With any luck, they will not be alerted to our presence by their systems."

Yeah, I could imagine an unauthorized spaceship docking at your station might set off alarms.

"However, if anyone in there is awake and looking out a window, there's nothing I can do about that."

I bit my lip. So until we sneaked in, we had no way of knowing who was there, or how prepared they were to greet us.

And that was before you thought about the fact that we were doing exactly what the Shepherds had wanted us to do. Dad and Nate were bait, and we were bringing Dr. Underberg to the station to rescue them.

Dr. Underberg tapped the control panel and brought up a diagram of the station. "I know from experience that animals brought up in stasis are kept in this module." He pointed at one of the areas in the lower stem. "That's your best bet for finding your father and Nate Noland."

"Wait, they're still asleep?" Savannah asked.

"I can't imagine why they'd wake them up," said Dr. Underberg. "You don't usually give hostages a tour of your space station."

She shook her head. "How are we supposed to get them off the station?"

"They'll be weightless," Howard said. "We'll push."

She looked appalled. "But they won't be naked, right? Gillian's mom was naked."

"I've seen Nate naked," said Howard. "It's not a big deal."

"Eww, shut up," Savannah said.

I puffed out my breath in frustration. If they were naked, they were naked. I wasn't wasting time risking the chance to save their lives to find them clothes before I sneaked them off the station. "We can take blankets or something and wrap them up like mummies."

"That's a great idea," said Howard. "It'll keep their limbs from flailing around, too. We can even use the sleep sacks."

I smiled at him, grateful that someone was thinking this through. Astronauts practiced every maneuver they'd ever have to perform on flight simulators for months in advance. Mission control prepared for every possibility. We were just going by feel, and it showed.

I suddenly had a terrible thought. "What if they do catch us? You can't protect yourself in here, can you?"

"Don't worry," said Dr. Underberg. "If there is one thing I am good at, it's heeding my survival instincts. Now, go down to the hatch on the third level. It will unlock when I've successfully docked at Infinity Base. I'll lock the door behind you when you head through the entrance, and unlock it when you return with your missing friends."

"How will you know when that is?"

"I've got a camera that can see whatever comes through that air lock," he said, his tone frank. "I'll know whether or not it's safe to open the door. Now, move along. Remember: timing is everything."

We were dismissed. We headed down as instructed, and Howard rolled up two sleeping sacks and stuck them in the pockets of his utility suit. While we waited near the hatch, Eric floated up to me.

"You know what he means by heeding his survival

instincts, right, Gills?" he asked, his tone concerned.

I looked at my brother.

"He means if things go wrong, he's definitely going to detach and leave us there."

I bit my lip.

"You know, or croak in the next five minutes. The only thing really keeping us safe is that the Shepherds want to use us as leverage for Dr. Underberg. No Dr. Underberg, no reason to keep us around at all."

I shuddered.

"I can still hear you, by the way." Dr. Underberg's voice floated through the cabin.

I glared at my brother. Great. And Eric just said "croak."

"But you're not wrong," the old man added. "I shall endeavor, then, to stay alive. For all of your sakes. Docking procedure complete."

The lights around the hatch turned green. Just beyond this door was the air lock to Infinity Base. And Dad. I'd almost made it.

Howard opened the hatch and we floated through.

I could immediately tell the difference. The air here was cleaner, fresher, like a mountain forest. The short, accordion-like tunnel we traveled through was sparkling clean. At the other end was a second hatch, through which shone a bright light that looked almost like daylight. And beyond that, the mission. I looked over my shoulder at the others, who nodded silently, waiting. We'd have to be quick. We'd have to be sneaky. It was probably impossible.

But it was our only chance.

I took a deep breath and reached for the lever to open the hatch.

It flew open, and Nate's face appeared in the portal. "Hi there!" he called, grinning. "Welcome to Infinity Base!"

GREETINGS, EARTHLINGS

FOR A LONG MOMENT, WE JUST STARED AT HIM. NATE NOLAND WAS SUP-posed to be unconscious, and possibly naked, and desperately glad that we'd come to rescue him. Instead, he looked like we'd dropped by with pizza. Good pizza, too, not the kind from General Tso's.

He was dressed in a soft, loose-fitting pair of dark pants, a V-neck sweater with an infinity sign embroidered above his heart, and a pair of soft slippers with little turned-up toes like elf shoes.

"Guys?" Nate said. "In or out? I can't keep the door open or outer space will get in. Probably."

"Nate!" Howard shoved me aside and pushed to the

front, but he didn't seem to know what to do when he got there. His brother clapped him on the shoulder and he found his tongue. "You're okay!"

Was he? I stared, confused. He seemed . . . happy. Which was an odd way to be if you were kidnapped, drugged, put into hypothermic torpor, and shot into space.

"I'm awesome, Howard. And you're right. This space thing is a blast. I can see why you wanted to come up here so badly. Seriously, though, in or out, I'm recommending in, because it's so cool in here, you have no idea."

We all came through the portal, and entered a small-ish chamber that looked a lot like the one we had just left, except far sleeker. Everything shone and glistened, and the mountain-fresh scent grew stronger. The lights here were bright as a sunny day and as my eyes adjusted to the room, I even saw green plants tucked into nooks and crannies.

I watched Nate warily. "Are you sure you're all right, Nate?"

Nate just grinned harder. "Of course I am. I mean, I wasn't. I was super scared when I woke up on a space station, but I'm trying to look on the bright side."

"The bright side?" Eric asked.

"I have something really great to write in my college entrance essays, right?" The smile was hopeful. Almost pleading.

Definitely scary.

"But . . . we came here to rescue you," Savannah said, baffled.

"Aww, Savvy. That's sweet. But really, I'm just glad you're here. We knew you were coming, you see."

"Who is *we*?" I pounced. "My dad?"

"Yeah," he said. "And Anton. You met Anton at dinner, he said, gee . . . how many days ago was it now?" He shrugged, which sent him floating across the room. "Anyway, he's great. Want to see him?"

No. And Anton was *not* great. I stayed put, hand firmly on one of the glossy handholds. "Anton is a Shepherd. And, you know, he kidnapped you. You were kidnapped."

And we were caught. We were caught before we even set foot on the station. This wasn't how any of this was supposed to go!

"No, I wasn't," Nate said.

"You were," said Savannah. "Gillian's mom said you had to fight them off."

Nate's smile faltered for a minute.

"In the car?" Savannah said. "Do you remember getting attacked in the car?"

Nate paused, and glanced over at the door he was herding us toward. "Wait until you see all the cool stuff on this space station, guys. I really think you'll like it. I certainly did."

"Like what?" Howard piped up, as if he didn't have a care in the world.

"Oh," said Nate half-heartedly. "You know. Plants, and animals . . . it's really cool."

No. Nothing here was cool. Something was very wrong. Nate wasn't acting like himself at all. Did he even remember getting attacked?

My mind reeled with possibilities, each more horrible than the last. Nate was lying to us. Nate was brainwashed. Nate was under strict instructions not to tell us the truth and that's why it was him and not my father here to greet us. Dad was somewhere else. Dad hadn't survived the journey . . .

A lump rose in my throat. "Where's my dad?"

"He's inside." He pointed at the door at the end of the module.

"Then why doesn't he come here?" I asked. "I don't want to see the space station."

"I do!" exclaimed Howard. "Come on, Gillian. Nate says it's fine." He pushed past me and floated toward the door.

Nate beckoned to the rest of us.

I shook my head and edged backward. "If Dad were awake, he'd come and greet us." After all, we'd blasted into space for him. I glanced behind me, at the air lock. Any minute now, Dr. Underberg was going to realize we'd been trapped, and he was going to disconnect and leave us here.

"Oh," said Nate. "Well, he's been kind of sick."

"Sick?" Eric asked.

"Dizzy," said Nate. "You know. From the microgravity. So he likes to stay in the wheel parts of the station." He brightened. "You guys have to check out the wheels. It's so cool. It's like those videos of the moon . . ." He trailed off and looked from Howard, hovering near the door, to the rest of us, still crowded around the air lock. "I really think you ought to listen to me."

This time, no one moved.

Howard looked longingly at the door, then back at us. "What are we waiting for?"

Nate flinched. "They aren't as easy to convince as you, Howard."

That seemed like the most honest thing he'd said so far.

"Not after the things we've seen," I said.

"And the things we know Anton has done," Savannah added. "You didn't see it, Nate. He's killed, like, millions of honeybees. I mean, designed them to die. He's a complete loon."

"He's a Shepherd," I finished. It was the same thing.

Nate watched us, then took a deep breath, as if coming to a decision. "Hey, remember when we were all trapped in Omega City and there were those guys chasing us?"

We nodded.

"And we ran away?"

"Yeah?" I put my hand on my hip in impatience.

He drifted closer. "That's because we *could* run away. There were places to run to. A whole big underground city. That's not the case here."

I narrowed my eyes as he leaned in closer and dropped his voice to a whisper.

"There's nowhere to run."

"Nate?" A note of confusion had entered Howard's voice.

My breath caught in my throat. It was true. We could get back on the ship, assuming Dr. Underberg would let us in, but I couldn't go and leave my father behind.

"So," Nate finished, the brittle smile in place as he drew back and resumed his normal speaking voice, "why don't you all come and meet Anton, and hear what he has to say? He's been really, really excited about the idea." He nodded and looked at us meaningfully.

And his meaning was achingly clear. We didn't have a choice. None of us.

I glanced at my brother, who sighed. "Right. Anton." He floated toward the door. "This space trip is great. I come half a million miles from Earth to escape the Shepherds, and here they are."

"Well, yeah," said Howard. "This is a Shepherd

station. Plus, we're only about two hundred and fifty miles up."

"Okay," Eric mumbled as Nate opened the door. Savannah gripped my shoulder hard.

"Though we did come pretty far to get here."

One by one, we floated through the door, with Nate bringing up the rear.

"We're circling the Earth once every hour and a half, so I guess you're right, it has probably been half a million miles, given all the hours we were in orbit last night."

His chatter seemed to come from very far away. I was breathing hard and heavy as I emerged into the next room.

This chamber was even bigger than the first, and instead of the analog dials, switches, and monitors of *Wisdom*, it was dominated by touch screens of all shapes and sizes, sleeping berths, and treadmills and other exercise equipment hanging out at all angles.

And floating in the middle of it, looking even more giant than usual in the cramped quarters, was Anton Everett. He smiled broadly at us.

"Hey there! Welcome to Infinity Base! I've been waiting for you guys to show up ever since I heard from home about the little mishap in Omega City. What a shock it was to discover you weren't on board with me."

A shock? Maybe he'd been surprised, but I was sure that wasn't his only reaction. Anger, probably. Frustration.

But none of that was evident in his behavior right now. He seemed as thrilled to see us as he had been back in Eureka Cove a few days ago. And I was positive he was faking it just as hard.

"And such a disappointment, too. I had so much to show you." He shook his head as if marveling at us. "You know, all this time I thought my Shepherd upbringing made me special, but look at you four. I didn't even get to go into space at your age. Mostly because the radiation and zero g isn't great for developing bodies, but it's kind of late to worry about that now, right?"

We all just stared at him, baffled.

Finally, I found my voice. "What's going on?"

Anton stopped and tilted his head. "Well, I don't know, Gillian. You're the one who has come to my space station. Why don't you tell me?"

"We're here to rescue my father and Nate."

"Excellent idea! Very brave. If risky." He floated a few feet away and tapped another screen. "After all, you had no idea what to expect when you got here. Did you?" He turned around and gave us another friendly grin.

This guy was either completely nuts, or the happiest kidnapper of all time. And the worst part was, I had no idea which one it was. Were we his prisoners or his pals?

"But, then again, that's what makes me think you guys

really have what it takes. Bravery. Resourcefulness. *Loyalty.* You know?"

"Have what it takes for what?" Howard asked.

"To make the hard choices in this world, Howard," Anton said. "To really look at the problems we're facing, and know what to do to save the human race."

Savannah's mouth was open. "Can we go back to the part about the radiation?"

"There's a ton of radiation in space," Howard said. "We have radiation shields on the rocket, but we still get bombarded with way more than we did back on Earth. Still, it won't be a problem as long as we're not up here too long."

"Yes, and Infinity Base is even better than those old rockets." Anton waved a hand at the docking bay dismissively. "We've done a lot of research into the subject. After all, our goal here is to serve as a launching pad for permanent missions into the cosmos. Don't worry—I'll give you the full tour soon enough."

"We don't want a tour," I said. "We want to get my father and go back to our ship."

"Underberg's ship," Anton corrected. "It was very good of you to bring him here." His eyebrows lifted curiously. "Where is Dr. Underberg, by the way?"

Back on the rocket. Possibly dying. But I wasn't about

to tell any of that to the Shepherd floating in front of me. After all, this was Anton Everett, the man who was personally responsible for the death of millions of bees. The only reason he was here was to get Underberg. At least if we kept him talking, we could delay that.

"What are you talking about?" Savannah said, her voice calm and even. "Underberg's gone. We came here on a ship we stole from Omega City." She stared at him, unblinking for a second, while the rest of us were too shocked to say anything. Even Howard didn't correct her.

But Anton merely chuckled. "Not bad. You'll still need some work, though, before you'll be ready to sell those lies. The bit about mixing the truth in is key. I'm very pleased to see you've already figured that part out. You'll make an excellent Shepherd."

Savannah glanced toward me, horrified.

Even without the benefit of gravity, my heart sank in my chest. If Savannah couldn't convince him, I don't know what hope any of the rest of us had.

That's what this was all about. Anton still thought he could recruit us. But this time, without all the niceties of a fancy dinner at Eureka Cove, or the illusion that we were free to just say no and walk away. Nate was right. We were trapped on this space station, trapped with *him*. Anton didn't have to play prison guard or keep us under lock and key. This was outer space. Our ships were our only way off the station, and Dr. Underberg had made it quite clear he would only open them if he thought it was safe.

Anton looked behind us, toward the outer chamber, and ran a hand through his salt-and-pepper hair. Even though the chamber was large, he seemed to fill it. I doubted he'd even fit inside *Knowledge* or *Wisdom*. I remembered reading somewhere that astronauts were usually short, like pilots, which was better both for resource management and for the cramped confines of space habitats. With his extraordinary height, Anton would never have been able to be an astronaut for NASA.

"Clever man, though, sending you out here alone. He's sealed himself off out here, has he? Let me guess: He told you he'd open the doors when you came back with your friends?"

We didn't say anything, but that appeared to be answer enough for Anton.

"Did he give you a password or anything? I know he still has the ability to watch us and see what we're doing." He looked at each of us in turn. "No? Well, that makes this all a little complicated."

"What?" I asked. "Killing him?"

"*Talking* to him," corrected Anton. "No one in our organization has tried honestly talking to Underberg in years. And I think he can be reasoned with. Diplomacy is always a better answer than violence, don't you think?"

"Yes," Nate said quickly. I gave him a nervous glance. Was this how we were all supposed to be acting?

"And I read your father's book. I think our aims are much more similar than Elana believes. We all want what is best for the world, right? I think we can still come to a mutually beneficial arrangement."

Fat chance, bee killer. But, following Nate's lead, I kept silent.

Anton wasn't done. "And, unlike Elana, I feel like we didn't really give any of you a fair shake back at Eureka Cove. I mean, wouldn't you say that? That we've gotten off on the wrong foot?"

"That's one way to put it," said Eric.

"I think once you really see the importance of what we're working on, you won't be so negative. Just ask Nate! He's been listening to me for a few days now and he's very excited."

"Very excited," Nate echoed, his teeth clenched. He nodded enthusiastically at us, as if begging us to play along.

I shook my head back. How anyone thought I'd be on the side of people who'd been hurting us for years was beyond me.

"I definitely think you guys should hear him out," Nate said quickly. "I mean, just a for a few minutes. You don't have to make any final decisions straightaway . . . um, right, Anton?"

"Right!" Anton exclaimed. "I'm in no particular rush. It's not as if any of us are going anywhere . . . are we?"

I shivered. Nope. Another plan in the dust. Eric had it correct. Five hundred thousand miles, and we were back where we started.

Prisoners of the Shepherds.

FALSE FLOCKS

ERIC WAS ALSO THE FIRST TO START PLAYING ALONG. "SURE," HE MUR-mured slowly, in his best fake-happy voice. "I suppose it wouldn't hurt to, you know, listen to Anton for a few minutes, Gills."

"And then you can go see your father," Anton added.

That got my attention. "Did you manage to recruit him, too?"

Anton cleared his throat, then pasted his smile back on. "What I did was try my best to *explain* things to him. Up here, away from all the distractions on Earth."

Away from all the escape routes, he meant.

"I will say, he was incredibly impressed to see everything

we've created up here. Truly stunned."

I didn't like the sound of that. "I want to see him now. First. Is he okay?"

Nate made a face. "Well . . ."

I glared at Anton. What had he done to my father?

"He's fine!" Anton said quickly. I must have looked panicked. "He's . . . well, let's just say he doesn't have a future in aeronautics."

"He hasn't stopped throwing up since he woke up," Nate added.

Howard shook his head. "He would have been kicked out of the space program for that. Not being able to tolerate weightlessness is an automatic cause for grounding." He turned to me. "Does he have a problem with his inner ear?"

I bristled. I didn't know. And it wasn't like Dad had asked to come to space, either. "Where is he?"

"I've been weaning him in the centrifuge rings," Anton explained. "He seems to do a little bit better in there. But actually, last I checked, I think he moved to the observation cupola to watch your approach."

I couldn't believe it. When I'd been staring out at Infinity Base, he'd been staring back. I'd spent the last day worrying about what they might do to him up here, and he'd spent it knowing we were walking into a trap.

The world narrowed to a single point. "I'm not doing anything until I see my father."

"Gillian . . . ," Nate said, his tone one of warning.

"No problem," Anton announced. "You've come such a long way. Of course you want to see your dad." He spread his arms wide. "And no one is in any rush here, after all. You aren't going anywhere."

His words were even creepier the second time around. I swallowed. We'd see about that once we had my father.

Anton smirked, as if he could read my mind. "I may not be able to open the hatch to Underberg's ship, but I can prevent him from releasing the docking lock. He'll be sticking around Infinity Base for the time being."

I tried to keep the disappointment from showing on my face. We could tackle getting the rocket ships loose later. Dad came first.

Anton motioned us toward the far exit, which stood open. "I think just Eric and Gillian to start. I'm sure Howard and Savannah would like to catch up with Nate. Plus, it'll be easier to keep my eyes on just the two of you." His tone was light and friendly, but we all knew debate was not an option. Savannah nodded at me and drifted closer to Nate. I didn't know what they'd discuss once we were gone. I wasn't sure they could even talk freely in here. This whole place was probably bugged. With one last look at the three of them, I floated after Eric and Anton in the passageway.

A long corridor connected the cylinders, with view ports at regular intervals showing glimpses of solar arrays and space, and hatches along its length, leading like a series of train cars into each chamber.

As we came closer to the far end of the station, I heard the hum of whatever motor turned the rings.

"Each ring turns at a rate of one and a half rotations per minute, or one point five rpm." Anton pointed at the smallest ring, turning just beyond the edge of the stem. "As each ring has a larger diameter, the artificial gravity within them is stronger the larger they get. This one is about a sixth of Earth's gravity, similar to the moon. We call it the bounce house."

I didn't want the tour. I just wanted Dad. I rushed through the corridor until we reached the final hatch.

"This is the observation cupola," Anton said, still acting like our official tour guide. I couldn't tell how much of his attitude was fake, and it creeped me out. "It's a bit of a boondoggle. There's really no practical purpose for so much wasted space. Not to mention the astronomical cost and trouble of installing wide-set glass portals. It wasn't in Underberg's original design. I'm sure he would agree with me that it's a weak spot on the station. But Elana wouldn't hear of it any other way. She didn't want a space station without a view, as she said. . . ."

I stopped listening and pulled the lever. The door opened with its usual pop and whoosh, and I floated through without another word.

I was surrounded by the universe. Stars—hundreds of thousands of stars, as far as the eye could see. More than I'd ever seen at night, even far out in the country. More than any planetarium. And unlike on Earth, the stars didn't twinkle. They were just sharp points of light. I could detect the bright, crowded curve of the Milky Way, the faint glow of reddish purple near the horizon of the hazy blue Earth, and brilliant white and pale-colored stars shining through it all. Huge glass panels arced over my head, the banded metal frames hardly breaking the view. At the very edges lay the rotating grayish curves of the centrifuge rings, and the occasional reception dish, but most of the room was filled with the vastness of space itself.

But I only spared a moment for the view Elana Mero had considered so very important. I didn't even care about the stars. Because in the middle of it all sat my father, on a soft sort of platform jutting out from the wall. His back was straight and he, too, was staring out into the blackness beyond. He was wearing the same soft, dark pajamas as Nate and Anton.

"Dad!" I shouted.

He turned, slowly, and looked back at me. "Gillian!"

I shoved off the threshold and went flying toward him. He seemed to be belted in but he caught me as I came whooshing past, folding me into his lap like I was no bigger than a baby. I threw my arms around him and buried my face in his chest.

"Dad. Dad. Dad." My eyes got blurry with tears that didn't fall in microgravity, no matter how hard I blinked. His hand was in my hair, and he was holding me so tight I couldn't breathe and didn't care. "We got you. We got you."

"Shhhh," he said. "Shhhh, it's okay."

And, for a single second, it was.

I lifted my head to look at my father, and realized my tears were still clouding my vision. Crying didn't work in space. I reached up to wipe the bubble of water from my lashes.

Distantly, I saw Eric floating through the hatch to join us. He piled into the hug, and I was grateful for the weight-lessness, as we all held on tight, three bodies with our own special gravity, pulling us into one great mass.

"You're here. You're both here? And you're all right?"

"We're great, Dad," said Eric, his voice muffled from being pressed up against us. "We're great."

"We found you."

"What happened here, Eric?" Dad touched the cut on his eyebrow.

"What do you think?" I asked. "Wild times in zero g."

Dad chuckled, stroked my brother's hair, squeezed me tighter, rubbed my back, and squeezed us all again. Then he held us both at arm's length, bobbing before him like a pair of twin satellites, and studied us. "I can't believe you came to outer space for me."

I came in again for another hug. "Believe it, Dad. I love you. To the moon and back."

It was the *back* part I was worried about.

But there was plenty of time for that. After all, Anton was right; there was no rush. I'd come half a million miles for this moment, and even if we were caught in another trap, this time we were here together.

Dad and Eric and I just sat there for a several minutes, holding each other and looking out over the cosmos. I wondered if these windows were bad for those cosmic rays Anton and Savannah had been talking about.

I turned my head to see if Anton was watching us from the door, but he seemed to have gone. Probably back to the others, to continue with his recruitment efforts. Or maybe to figure out how to get to Dr. Underberg.

I sat up. "Dad, what are we going to do?"

Dad sighed and stared beyond me into the blackness. "I'm not sure yet. Anton—well, you know what Anton thinks, right? He's determined to *give us another chance*." Dad's mouth twisted on the words, as if they were sour.

I could only imagine what my father thought about joining a massive conspiracy. They clearly didn't know him at all, if they thought he might.

"Can he hear us?" I asked.

Dad kept his voice low. "I don't know. His equipment

would have to be very good, with all the sounds of the machinery and life-support systems. But I think if he wanted to listen, he could have just stayed here. It's not like we could have kicked him out."

No. We didn't have a choice about anything on Infinity Base, and Anton knew it.

"And I've advised Nate to play along." At the look on my face, he added, "We have to learn more about what we're up against, and what the Shepherds really want. From us, from Underberg, all of it."

"Nate's been doing a great job," Eric said. "He really scared me for a while."

I nodded. "I thought he'd been brainwashed at first."

Dad shook his head. "You shouldn't have come, Gillian. This isn't like Omega City—"

"But Dad—" I broke in. "We couldn't leave you here."

"And it wasn't like we were safe back on Earth," Eric pointed out under his breath. "The Shepherds would have found us. They already had Mom and Dani."

"Right," Dad said slowly. "Where is your mother?"

I looked down at my knees, folded up under the stretchy straps holding us to the platform.

"She was taken," Eric said. "When we were trying to launch the rocket ship. We hid, like she asked us to."

I toyed with the flaps on my utility suit. Yeah, and then, instead of going after her, we'd blasted off to save Dad and

Nate. "But Dani said they'd be okay . . . sort of. When they were captured."

"So the Shepherds took both your mom and Dani Alcestis?" Dad asked. "Explain to me about Dani? Anton says she thinks she's Dr. Underberg's daughter, and has turned against the Shepherds to align herself with Underberg."

"He told you all that?"

"He doesn't have much of a filter. He's a purist. A bit like Howard, actually."

I wrinkled my nose. "He's nothing like Howard."

"I meant that he thinks what he thinks and is baffled by the idea that anyone could hear his arguments and not agree. He's not afraid to lay all his cards on the table. What he wants from us, what he wants for the world, even how he disagrees with his boss, Elana. If both he and Dani are having doubts about the Shepherds' goals, that might work in our favor."

"I don't know if Dani really has turned against the Shepherds," I said. "She seems to agree with everything they do, except she doesn't want them to kill her father. Or us. She was the one who helped us escape."

"What makes her think she's Underberg's daughter?" Dad asked. "I never ran across any mention of a family in all my Underberg research."

"But you didn't ask the Shepherds," I said. "To be fair."

Dad hadn't even figured out that Underberg had been a Shepherd.

Dad chuckled at that. "You're going to end up a better researcher than I am."

"Believe it, Dad," said Eric. "They've been communicating through radio codes for months. We saw all these old photo albums in her house with pictures of Underberg and her mother. Dr. Underberg even made the key to his spaceship based on a geometrical puzzle he and her mom used to write love letters to each other."

"Now that I have to see." His eyes shone as he looked down at me. I could almost picture a follow-up to his infamous biography. *Underberg: The Shepherd Years.*

That was, if we ever saw home again.

"Anton scares me," I said.

"Me too, kiddo. He's a true believer in the Shepherd cause. But we can use that to our benefit."

"How?"

"True believers want nothing more than for other people to believe what they do."

"Sound familiar, Gills?" Eric drawled.

"Shut up," I said. "This is different. This isn't about helping people see hidden facts. It's about the way he wants the world to be." It was what the Shepherds had been raised to believe—there was no right except what got them what they wanted, no wrong but what wrecked their plans. It was hard to fight against something like that, or trust that even the seemingly good things they wanted—like this beautiful space station—were for the right reasons.

After all, hadn't Elana said she'd destroy Infinity Base if it would protect her interests at Guidant?

"Gillian's right." Dad nodded solemnly. "And we're lucky that Anton not only believes what he does, but that he also thinks we're valuable to that system. In his opinion, he's giving us one last chance to make the right choice. To become Shepherds."

I looked through the glass. There, at the very edges, I could see a sliver of Earth.

Back on the surface, I'd aligned myself with Dani, because as weird and prickly as she was, she was also better than being captured by the Shepherds. Here, Dad wanted me to play along with Anton Everett, who might be verifiably insane, because the alternative was . . . what? Getting frozen? Getting killed? Getting shot out of an air lock into the vacuum of space?

"But where does it end?" Eric asked. "If we say we're on his side, if we make him believe it, will he take us back to Earth? Will they let Mom go?"

"I don't know the answer to that," Dad said. "But I've been racking my brain ever since I woke up here, and I can't think of any other option. Up here, we're at his mercy. If we can get back to Earth, we might stand a better chance."

Eric made a face. *"Join us or die,"* he said in a scary movie voice.

Except this wasn't a movie. We weren't Luke Skywalker facing off against Darth Vader. We didn't have glowing laser swords or magical powers. I wasn't even a particularly good liar.

"Do you think you can do it, Gillian?" Dad asked. "Play along? At least until we get home?"

Where did that leave Dr. Underberg? "I don't know. The Shepherds have hurt us so much, for so long . . . are we supposed to say we've forgotten all of that?"

"If our lives depend on it?" Eric asked. "Yes. Look at it this way, Gills. You always want to know the truth about everything. Well, the Shepherds are the ones who have it."

He had a point there. "So we'd say we want to join the Shepherds . . . to finally have all the secrets?"

"Something like that," Dad said. "It's not like I'm a scientist."

"But what about the others?" I asked. "Sav can probably figure out how to lie, but what about Howard?"

"I thought of that," Dad admitted. "But Nate has a plan there. He believes focusing on the benefits of this space station will be enough to make Howard seem enthusiastic."

That was for sure.

"And this space station *is* quite incredible. That's an

objective fact. Anton is dying to show it off to you."

I could believe that. "You should have seen all his crazy experiments back at Eureka Cove, Dad."

Eric nodded. "Chimps and bugs and bees . . . I fell into a tank full of flesh-eating beetles!"

"*Dead* flesh," I clarified. "He didn't even get bit."

"That doesn't make it okay!" he shot back.

Dad squeezed us both. "I believe it."

It was so nice to have Dad back. Real Dad, who believed the wild stories and understood when we did the right thing, even if it wasn't the safest thing in the world. "You don't know what we've been through. What the Shepherds are doing."

"I'm beginning to get a sense," he replied. "I just . . . I don't think I've ever dealt with a conspiracy quite this large before. A whole secret space station?" He shook his head. "I can't imagine the lengths one has to go to, to hide a creation of this magnitude from every government on Earth."

"From every astronomer, too," I said. "Dani told us that any time someone uses a Guidant program for their data or their photos—"

"Did you have a nice reunion?" said a voice at our back. We turned to watch Anton floating toward us, his calm smile making me want to adjust the settings on my utility suit to control my chills.

"Very nice," my father said. "I appreciate the chance to

show my children this extraordinary sight."

Anton's gaze rose to the stars surrounding us. "It is quite beautiful. I never spend much time here myself. I'm much more interested in the technical side of the base. I can't wait to show you my experiments up here. I gather from the others you got quite an in-depth view of my work back in Eureka Cove?"

I looked at Eric. He looked at me. Neither of us said anything. We were never going to be able to pull this off.

"Don't worry, you won't offend me," Anton added jovially. "Your friend Savannah has already shared her . . . intense criticism regarding the unfortunate incident with the bees."

"She—she has?" Oh, no. Were we sunk before we even got started?

"Yes. And she's not the first. I made a terrible error in judgment there. I'm not afraid to admit when I'm wrong. I just wish I'd realized it sooner."

"Before you killed all those bees?"

"Before we devoted so many resources to a futile effort," he said. "It turns out people don't really care about honeybees. It's too small. Too subtle. Like global warming. I promise, the next time we make people think the world is ending, it'll be something big and fiery. Something they can't possibly ignore."

Yeah, I definitely needed to turn up the heat on my suit.

HIDDEN FIGURES

ANTON REALLY WAS QUITE THE SHEPHERD. WITHIN MOMENTS, HE'D gathered us all up and herded us out of the observatory and back into the long train of chambers that made up the main stem of the station.

"I think it's probably time to go check on Dr. Underberg, don't you think, Gillian?"

"Um . . ." I was still dumbfounded, fighting to regain the power of speech after Anton's shocking announcement. I shuddered to think of what kind of big, fiery thing the Shepherds would use to try to convince the people of Earth that the world was ending. If they really did have the power to alter astronomical data, they could simply invent an asteroid coming to hit the Earth. That would scare millions. Terrify the entire population of the Earth enough to listen to anything—absolutely anything—that the Shepherds wanted them to.

And we would be a part of it.

We all floated effortlessly through the cabins, but not Dad. He lurched, awkward, from handhold to handhold, looking green the whole time. "Go slower," he begged. "This microgravity doesn't suit me."

"Take your time, Sam," Anton said. "It's not like we'll be far away. You can't get too far away from anyone on Infinity Base." His tone was pleasant, but there was no mistaking his words. It was a threat.

I cast a look behind me at my father, who was clenching his jaw as the space grew between us. He met my eyes, and nodded slightly.

Play the game. Lie like a Shepherd.

I wasn't certain that I could, but I knew one thing for sure—if I pulled this off, then the second I got back to Earth, I wouldn't stop until everyone in the world knew what kind of liars they were.

"I've been trying to open a channel of communication to Underberg," Anton was explaining to us. "But he refuses to respond. Still, I know he is receiving my messages, even if he won't talk to me." He ushered us through the door back into the entrance chamber. "Or undo the latch."

"Gillian!" Savannah called. She was gripping a handle near the air lock. "Did you see your father? Is he all right?"

"He's fine," I said. "It's like Nate told us. He's just a little . . . spacesick. How are you guys?" Savannah was probably wishing she'd stayed back on Earth like she'd wanted to.

"I'm . . . adjusting," Savannah said, her expression sour. "Anton really wants Dr. Underberg to open the door."

"But he won't," Howard announced.

"Indeed," Anton broke in. "I was hoping your presence might make a difference, Miss Seagret. Would you care to enter the air lock and give it your best shot?"

"Um . . ." I looked at Eric. "Alone?"

What if this was some kind of trick, and Anton wanted me in the air lock so he could manipulate Dr. Underberg? Eric's *join us or die* joke didn't seem very funny. Anton could easily threaten to make Dr. Underberg open the door or unseal the locks, pushing me out into space.

"Of course not," Anton said, looking confused. "I'll be going in, too."

"Why?" I asked, my voice shaky.

"So I can meet Dr.—" Realization dawned on his features. "Gillian, do you think I want to hurt you?"

"No," I said. *Yes. Absolutely.*

"If I wanted to hurt you, to hurt any of you, I'd have done it already. I know where everything is on this station,

I knew you were coming, I even had two of you uncon- scious, in my care. Hurt you? Don't be silly! I want to *help* you. *All* of you, including the stubborn old man in there." He pointed out the air lock. "And it would be a big help to me right now if you went with me and helped convince him of that fact. I've read your father's book. Dr. Under- berg trusts you. He trusts you enough to bring you here. And now *you* are going to get him to trust *me*."

Again, I was herded by the Shepherd, this time right into the tiny air lock. Anton was massive next to me in the crowded space. Nervously, I maneuvered over to the door to *Wisdom*, careful not to touch him. He hooked the upturned toe of his slipper around a handle set in the floor and appeared to be standing, casually, arms crossed, like he was lining up at the post office.

I stared down at his feet. "So that's what the elf toes are for."

Anton glanced down. "Oh, yeah. Do you want a pair?"

"No. I'll stick to my utility suit." At least I could trust it, unlike anything having to do with Anton. I looked at the closed hatch on *Wisdom*. "Do you want me to knock or something?"

"I've no doubt he's watching us. Just explain the situ- ation."

That's what I was afraid of. *Explain the situation.* We're the hostages of a lunatic, and we're all pretending everything is fine so he'll let us go back to Earth. Oh, and he's standing right behind me, so why don't you go ahead and give him complete access to your ship?

"Hey, Dr. Underberg," I said, wondering if I sounded as dumb as I felt. "Gillian here."

I waved, just in case maybe he was only getting a visual and not sound.

"We've got my dad and Nate." I counted them off on my fingers. "And they are totally okay." I made the scuba-diving symbol, with my index finger and thumb forming an O with the other three fingers straight up. "We're all fine here. Anton"—I pointed back at him—"has been very . . . welcoming."

I checked with Anton. He gave me a thumbs-up.

"And he wants you to open the door. So. You know. Could you?"

And then I stepped back. I hoped I'd sounded sincere enough for Anton. And I hoped Dr. Underberg was as suspicious as ever and didn't let us in.

A minute passed, and nothing happened. "Maybe he's asleep," I suggested to Anton. "He . . . falls asleep a lot."

"He's not asleep." Anton's tone had turned dark, and he pushed me aside. "He's impossible. Maybe Dani really is his daughter. It certainly would explain where she got her stubborn streak from."

I shrank back, scared both by the growl in his voice and

by how much space he took up in front of the little hatch. Anton may not want to hurt us, but he totally could.

Anton raised his fist and banged on the hatch. "Open up in there!"

I pushed myself backward as his shouts echoed around the tiny hatch. The air lock was as small as the inside of a car, and Anton took up most of the space.

"Um . . . ," I said softly, but he wasn't even listening.

"Don't you get it?" Anton screamed at the thick door. "I don't care about Elana's plan. I think whatever they did to you when I was a kid was an absolute waste! You had a lot to offer us. You still do, but you can't do it from in there!"

I glanced back through the air-lock door, where the others were gathered, peering in. Behind them, I saw my father, clinging awkwardly to the walls. I was pretty sure Anton's voice was carrying just fine.

Gingerly, I eased myself back into the room. I don't think Anton even noticed, because he was still shouting uselessly at Dr. Underberg's spaceship.

"You think I don't know exactly what's going on in there? I've seen the analyses you've done on your ship every time you pop in here to make repairs and steal supplies."

"Dad?" I squeaked. I gestured to the door on our end. Anton wasn't paying any attention to us. We could close the door right now. We could lock *Anton* in the air lock. Make him our prisoner.

"Your heat shields are damaged, your propulsion rockets are running at seventeen percent of normal, your air filtering is completely out of whack, and . . . come on, Aloysius. Let's be honest here. Not even *your* batteries have enough juice to get you back to Earth at this point. What choice do you have?"

Dad awkwardly clawed his way toward us. "Don't," he said softly, shaking his head.

"But this is our chance." I clasped my hands in front of me. "We could trap him."

"And then what?" Dad said. "We still can't get home if he's in between us and Underberg's ship. And even if we could, you heard him—Underberg doesn't have the power to get us back to Earth."

"But Shepherds lie!" I protested.

Anton had now resorted to cursing and kicking at the door with his soft slippers. I didn't think that would accomplish anything but bruising his feet.

"Do you think what Anton is saying about Underberg's ship is a lie?" Dad asked.

I hung my head. "Honestly?"

"No," said Howard. "It's a real wreck in there. *Wisdom*, though, maybe. The Shepherds fixed it all up."

And he wasn't the only one thinking of *Wisdom*. Anton had moved on to shouting about that, too. "You know I'm right, Aloysius! I personally overhauled your second ship from top to bottom for the past six months. I know exactly what kind of junk you've been flying around on here. You're lucky you haven't dropped out of the sky!"

Yikes.

"Okay," I said. "What about the shuttle you guys came up on?"

"Who would fly it?" Nate asked. "Howard?"

"Yes!" cried Howard.

"Shh!" we all warned him.

Howard clapped his mouth shut. "It doesn't matter, anyway. The real problem is the landing. You can't just land a spaceship like it's an airplane."

"You can't land an airplane, either, Howard," Nate pointed out.

"I don't know how the Guidant spacecraft lands," Howard said. "Does it parachute into some field like the Russian Soyuz capsule? Does it fall into the sea? You can't just land. You need a team on the ground to come get you."

The Shepherds. I sighed. Even if we got back to Earth, we still needed to play nice.

"Listen, while he's distracted," Dad said. "Are we all on the same page here? Nod and smile. Do your best to seem as if you're considering all his points. Don't overplay your hand—he's a genius—but don't argue with him too much."

"You should have seen Sav here go after him before

about bees or whatever," Nate said. "I thought we were all dead meat."

"That's good, though," Dad said. "If we all just immediately converted it would look suspicious. A little hesitation and uncertainty on our parts is realistic. Remember, the point is to get back home. Just keep your head down and pay attention."

"There is no down," Howard said. "We're in micro-gravity."

Savannah groaned.

"If you don't know what to say," Nate suggested, "ask him about the base. He can talk about it for hours."

I pursed my lips and gazed longingly at the air-lock door. Or we could skip all this pretense and just lock Anton in until he promised to send us home. My fingers itched to slam the door on him. I pictured laughing in triumph as he rushed back to us, his face pressed against the portal window.

But Dad was right. Then what? What if he refused to help us? We weren't about to leave him there to die. And whenever we did open the door again, we'd have lost any chance of getting him to trust us, to believe we were on the Shepherd side.

I pulled my hand back, balling it against the thigh of my utility suit. Maybe I was becoming more like a Shepherd than I thought.

ANTON YELLED AT the hatch of *Knowledge* for another five minutes, while we all stood there wondering what to do.

I shook my head. If only there were a way to get a message—a real message—to Dr. Underberg. But I didn't know if he could see us or just hear us, and we couldn't risk letting our guard down with Anton watching our every move.

I looked at Howard. "Do you remember how to make the ciphers? The number ciphers like Dani was using at Eureka Cove?"

"Yeah," he said, looking affronted that I would doubt him. "It's just an alphabet."

"Can you make one?" I asked.

"With what keyword?"

"Omega," I said quickly. That was the one Dr. Underberg used on the code book he'd given Howard.

Inside the air lock, Anton's tone had turned cajoling. "Don't you want to see the base without sneaking around?" he was asking Underberg. "I'm sure you haven't gotten a chance to really enjoy all the features."

Howard opened one of the pockets on his thigh and pulled out the space pen we'd gotten him for his birthday. Nate rolled up his shirtsleeve for Howard to write on his arm.

"What do you know?" Howard said. "It really does write in microgravity."

"Hurry," I said.

"What do you want it to say?"

I bit my lip. I didn't know. And I wasn't sure how we'd communicate it to him anyway. Tap it out, like Morse code?

"Make it say 'play along,'" Dad suggested. He looked at me and shrugged. "More allies couldn't hurt."

"Especially one who could actually land a spaceship," Eric added.

"Yeah, that's good." I toyed with the zipper pull on my suit. I was getting as bad as Howard. He painstakingly inked the code on his brother's wrist as I tried to think of ways to get a message to Dr. Underberg.

"Fine!" Anton snapped, then came shooting out of the air lock. I nearly gasped in surprise and quickly looked at Howard and Nate. Howard was still holding his pen, but Nate had pulled his sleeve back down.

"I'm not in any rush. He's only hurting himself in there. I can't imagine all the medical problems he's experiencing. I could help him, you know. We could wean him back onto gravity. We could put him in torpor and ship him back to Earth."

"You could lure him out in the open and then kill him, like the Shepherds have been trying to do for decades," I blurted, then clapped a hand over my mouth. I was going to suck at this lying thing.

But Anton merely sighed. "You're not wrong, Gillian. We really haven't given Underberg any reason to trust us, have we?"

Nate floated up behind me and bumped his arm against mine. I looked down.

	1	2	3	4	5
1	O	M	E	G	A
2	B	C	D	F	H
3	I	J	K	L	N
4	P	Q	R	S	T
5	U	V	W	Y	X/Z

41	34	15	54	15	34	11	35	14
P	L	A	Y	A	L	O	N	G

Oh my goodness. That was a lot of numbers.

Anton was still talking. "It's amazing he's even been communicating with Dani."

I was breathing heavy. Nine numbers. Big numbers.

"Yes," I said, raising my voice. Could Dr. Underberg hear us all the way in here? He had to be listening, especially after Anton's outburst. *"They were communicating. In code.* They had a code they used to send messages back and forth."

"Figures. Dani was always obsessed with codes. She and her mother used to do the same thing."

"Did she ever teach them to you?" I asked.

"Gillian," Dad warned.

"You were friends when you were kids, right?" I asked. "How old are you now? *Forty-one?*"

"Good guess."

I swallowed thickly. "And Dani has to be *thirty-four*, right?"

Nate stiffened beside me. I checked his arm again.

"She'd find that flattering. She's closer to—"

"She told us you dated." I barreled ahead. "How long? *Fifteen* years?"

Anton's expression turned grim. "We were together for a while, yes. But that doesn't make her betrayal okay. The Shepherds raised her, and look how she turned on us."

My voice was shaking. "She did it to save her father."

"She never even met him."

Focus, Gillian, focus. Nate put his arm around me, as if to steady me. I checked out the numbers again. "Well, he must have been *fifty-five* when she was born."

"He wasn't even around when she was born."

Five more. Just five more. "And she was *fifteen* when her mom died, right?"

Anton's eyes narrowed. "What are you doing?"

"Gillian!" Dad barked.

But I was too far gone. "I can't imagine what it's like for her. Down there. Alone. *Thirty-four . . .*"

Anton floated my way. "What are you—" He caught me by my clenched hands and pulled me away from Nate.

I saw Nate shoving his sleeve back into place as Anton wrenched open my fists as if they contained clues.

"What are these numbers?"

"Let go of her!" Dad cried.

"Eleven!" Howard shouted. "Thirty-five! Fourteen!"

Silence. Nothing but the sound of the machines whirring.

Anton regarded me carefully. "What did you say to him?"

"Nothing." I was still a terrible liar.

"What did you say?" he pressed.

My mouth was so dry I didn't know how I found my voice. "'Run away.'"

Anton dropped my hands in disgust. "That's the wrong number of letters, little Seagret. But you're getting better at deception. We'll make a Shepherd out of you yet."

No, They would not!

Dad rushed to my side. "Leave my children alone."

Anton laughed mirthlessly. "I've been nothing but good to your children, Sam. They're the ones who won't help *me*."

Just then, from inside the air lock, we heard a mechanical whir. The door to *Knowledge* was opening.

ARTIFICIAL GRAVITY

ANTON PEEKED IN THE AIR LOCK AND TURNED TO ME. "WELL, WHATEVER you said to him seems to have worked, Gillian. He's doing what I asked."

Oh, no. I felt sick to my stomach. What had I done?

"Care to introduce us?"

I looked at my father. "Dad has to come, too," I said. I didn't know what Anton had planned, but I hoped having backup would help.

"Of course," said Anton. "Sam knows more about this old man than anyone."

I looked at the others. Eric's and Savannah's faces were stricken with fear. Even Howard appeared wide-eyed and worried. Nate was rubbing his sleeve against his arm, clearly hoping to smudge Howard's writing in case Anton decided to inspect.

I took a deep, shuddering breath. What did *play along* mean to Dr. Underberg? What was I about to walk into?

The three of us floated back into Underberg's ship. As the sour, stale smell surrounded us, both Dad and Anton wrinkled their noses.

"I told you this place was falling to pieces," Anton said with a sniff.

I floated up through the lower chamber and into the command center, with Dad right behind me and Anton at his heels.

Dr. Underberg was staring down at his mess of screens, but his bald, emaciated head creaked upward and turned jerkily in our direction.

"Dr. Underberg, I presume?" Dad said, a smile playing across his lips.

"Dr. Seagret," Dr. Underberg stated, nodding, He turned his bleary gaze on Anton. "Shepherd."

"Anton Everett," Anton said, floating forward with his hand outstretched. "It's an honor to meet you, sir."

Dr. Underberg grunted, and didn't raise his hand. "Are you here to kill me?"

"No, sir. I think there's been a misunderstanding,"

"I understand everything, young man," he said.

"Especially all the things you were so good as to shout through my door. My ship's broken. *I'm* broken. And you weren't calling me sir then, were you? No, you were far more informal."

Anton had the decency to look contrite. "What do you want me to call you?"

"I don't want to speak to you at all."

"Then why did you open the door?" Anton asked. He looked at me accusingly, but I knew Dr. Underberg couldn't have gotten our code. Or if he had, he sure had a strange idea about what it meant to play along.

"Because you were attacking a little girl."

My eyes began to sting again. Elana had been right. Dr. Underberg would risk himself to save us.

"I wasn't going to hurt her. I don't want to hurt any of you. I believe you are too valuable to our cause."

"And what is your cause now, Shepherd?"

"What it's always been. Take humanity to the stars. We've built your space station. We've spent years developing species here and on Earth for long-term space habitation and travel."

"And you keep it all a secret from the very people you claim to be trying to help."

I looked at Dad, who was staring in silent wonderment, taking it all in.

"People aren't ready," Anton insisted. "They weren't

ready for Omega City then, they aren't ready for Infinity Base now. No one believes in what we do because they don't want to." He gestured to my father. "Do you know why it was easy to destroy this man's reputation? Because people would rather believe that people like us are crackpots than that the very survival of the human race is at risk."

I gasped. "That's not true! You never even give them a chance. Something like this space station? People would be in awe of it."

"And they will be," Anton said. "When the time is right."

"When will that be?" my father asked. "When the Shepherds manufacture some crisis that Guidant can profit from?"

Anton let out a bark of laughter. "You have it backward. Everything Guidant does is so that the Shepherds can work on their real goals."

"Not according to Elana," I said. "She told me that Shepherd goals are old-fashioned, and that Guidant is all that really matters."

"Well, Guidant is her pet project," said Anton, smugly placid. "And it's been very profitable. I can't argue with that. Without Guidant, we would never have had the money to build this space station. But Elana knows where the real priority lies. With our plans. With Infinity Base."

Elana didn't care about Infinity Base. She'd said so

herself. And I was about to tell Anton that when I noticed that Dr. Underberg had passed out again.

I shook my head sadly and gestured to him. "He keeps doing that," I said. "Is he dying?"

Anton pressed his fingers to the side of Dr. Underberg's neck, checking his pulse. "He's old," he said. "And microgravity is incredibly hard on human bodies in long periods, even if you do exercises to try to keep muscle tone. Radiation, bone density loss—and I have no idea what kind of physical shape he was in before he blasted off into space."

"You should let him rest," Dad suggested. "It's not like he's going anywhere."

Anton shrugged. "I suppose so. Elana really wants me to get this wrapped up, though, one way or another."

One way or another? I must have looked even more terrified, as Dad gave me a reassuring nod.

"He does this a lot," I said. "Fall asleep. I'm sure he'll be ready to talk some more in an hour or two."

Anton sighed. "In an hour or two could I count on getting more support from you? You're acting like I'm the enemy when what I'm really trying to do is save his life. Save all of you."

I thought about what Nate had said, how Anton would talk for hours about Infinity Base. Like Howard.

"Well, maybe it's hard to convince me because I don't

have a sense of what you're trying to do. Maybe it's hard to convince the world of all the good you're doing because all the Shepherds insist on keeping your work a secret. We can hardly support you if we don't know what you're doing."

Anton appeared to consider this, while behind him, Dad gave me a thumbs-up and an impressed smile. I breathed out heavily. I could do this. As long as I wasn't lying.

"Okay, Gillian," said Anton. "We'll let the old man sleep, and I'll show you some of my favorite parts of this station."

I looked at Dad, who held up his hands. "I've seen it."

"Can I bring the others?" I asked.

"Of course!" Anton said brightly. "The centrifugal rings are one of a kind. We're really proud of them."

But they'd kept them a secret from the whole world. Curious. I couldn't imagine anyone making something so amazing and then just keeping it a secret. Dr. Underberg had with Omega City, but he hadn't been given the choice. If people knew what the Shepherds had created up here, they would be admired all over the world. But instead they kept it a secret, and let Guidant distract us with stories of satellites and self-driving cars, just so they could choose what the rest of humanity was ready to see and hear.

It made no sense. I could pretend to be impressed by

the Shepherds, but there was no way I'd ever agree with their beliefs.

"I think . . . I'd like that," I said warily. "Let's go do it now."

Together, we eased back through the portals that led out of the ship. As I left *Knowledge*'s command center, I gave one last look to my father, who floated by Dr. Underberg's chair. And I may have been wrong, but for a second, I could have sworn the old man's eyes were open.

ONCE AGAIN, WE were in the long corridor that led underneath the cylindrical stem modules of Infinity Base. Anton led the way, with Howard close behind, peppering him with questions about the workings of the station. He'd clearly taken Nate's advice to heart. Or maybe he was just being his usual self.

I followed alongside Savannah, trying to find a way to communicate privately to her that Dr. Underberg and my dad were back on the ship, plotting . . . something. Eric and Nate were farther behind us, playing some kind of game on the walls and ceiling that looked like touch football, if everyone on the team were Spider-Man. They almost didn't look like prisoners.

Anton kept up a steady lecture. He managed to put even Howard's factoids to shame. "Microgravity is one of the most persistent problems with long-term space travel.

It's our main area of research here on Infinity Base. How to keep people healthy and hearty for long space trips."

I crossed my arms, which sent me pitching into the wall. "I know. I saw the skeletons of your chimpanzee test subjects." They'd been picked clean by tanks of beetles.

"Oh, that's right," Anton said offhandedly. "You saw everything on Eureka Cove. Of course, that was just the beta testing. We have the next level up on Infinity Base. Here, we're trying to prepare for the time when humans will live in space, either permanently, or during long-term travel to colonize other planets. Our dream is that, one day, Infinity Base will be the launch point for humanity's journey to a million stars."

Howard's eyes were so wide now, I was surprised they didn't pop out of his head. I had to admit, it sounded really nice, until you remembered how their space station was built on a pack of lies.

"So, the stuff we saw on the island. The chimps, and the sheep, and those . . . moths? They're tests?" Savannah asked.

"We breed species to be most efficient for human needs during space living. Sheep provide wool, milk, and even meat, but we need to keep them compact to fit in our habitats. Those moths spin silk in their larval form, then the adult form is an excellent source of protein."

"Eww," said Eric.

"And the chimps stand in for human test subjects. We study their bone density loss, the effects of space radiation on their offspring, and of course, the effects of long-term hypothermic torpor on their brain function."

"Eww," said Savannah.

Nate stopped playing for a second. "Wait, I have brain damage?"

"Most human studies of hypothermic torpor are done on people who have already experienced brain damage," Anton explained. "Hospitals use brain cooling to help drowning or suffocation victims minimize the damage that oxygen deprivation has already done to their brains. But there isn't a lot of data as to what it can do to normal brains."

"You're assuming Nate has a normal brain," said Eric.

"Hey!" said Nate, and shoved him lightly, though it was enough to send Eric tumbling head over heels down the hall.

"The good news is that our research on chimps seems to show that there's no permanent damage, even if they are kept in torpor for days or even weeks. They might have some temporary motor-skills issues when they first wake up, though. They may be uneasy walking, or a bit clumsier than usual."

"Ah, I don't even have that!" Nate proclaimed as Eric barreled into him from behind and the two of them went crashing into another wall.

Savannah clung to the floor. "Guys. Guys! We don't all have our space legs."

As soon as we'd all settled down, Anton stopped at a wide hatch some distance from the end of the corridor. "We'll all have to be quick getting inside here. There's a twenty-second window during each rotation. Oh, and go feetfirst."

"Why?" Savannah asked.

"You'll see in a minute." He looked at the indicator lights along the wall and pressed a button. The hatch opened wide with its usual pop. "Okay, go!"

We pulled ourselves through the hatch and found ourselves at a funnel-shaped end of a long tunnel about the width of a car. There were rungs set in one side, I assumed to help us pull ourselves along. Anton turned his feet in the direction of the end of the tunnel and started pulling himself down, end over end.

I floated forward a foot or two, watching him curiously. "What are you doing?"

But I guess I'd pushed myself harder than I thought, as I bumped into Anton's shoulder with my knee. He grabbed me harshly and slid me in the same direction as him.

"I said, feetfirst!"

"Okay!" I grabbed on to the rungs and was shocked to find myself still sliding downward. When I let go again, the rungs started moving up past my hands, like I was slowly sinking to the bottom of a swimming pool. I grabbed on to a rung and hung on.

Gravity had returned.

"This is so cool!" Eric cried as he slid past me on the far wall of the tunnel.

"Grab on to something! It only gets stronger as we go down!" Anton called down to him.

Because all of a sudden I could *tell* which way was down.

We weren't at the end of a tunnel. We were at the top of one. We were inside one of the huge spokes connecting the rings to the rest of the station. I stopped descending for a moment and closed my eyes, trying to see if I could feel the rotation, but then Savannah bumped into me from above.

Quickly, we maneuvered down the rungs, and eventually I even had to use my hands and feet and climb down like a ladder. I felt a little dizzy and disoriented as the pressure on my hands and feet grew stronger. I was getting heavier.

At last, we reached the floor. I hopped down the last few rungs and alighted a foot or two farther than I'd intended. So there was gravity, but not as much as normal. We were standing in a small, bare chamber with a door set in one end.

I bent my legs and did a tiny practice hop. At least, it

was supposed to be tiny. Instead of a few inches, I moved a foot and a half into the air, then dropped lightly back down. My hands shot out toward the rungs to steady myself. It felt weird and dreamlike, like falling through water or in slow motion.

When we'd all reached the ground, Anton crossed to the door. "This ring is my baby," he said, with obvious pride. "All my best work is in here."

His best work? I made a face. We'd already seen the bees. Did I really want to know what lay beyond that door?

With a flourish, he opened the hatch and stepped aside to let us through.

THE FOREST PRIMEVAL

I STEPPED OUT INTO THE CHAMBER, WHICH MUST HAVE BEEN THE INTE-
rior of the largest ring on the station. The hollow space
was curved, walls and ceiling stretching in a cylinder that
could have fit my entire house across without scraping
off the paint. And it was filled with trees. Trees, bushes,
undergrowth; an entire forest seemed to have sprung to life
inside this ring. The air was misty, and off in the distance
in either direction the ground rose as if up a hill.

High above, set into the ceiling, were bright lights,
casting the whole chamber in the rosy-white light of early
morning.

A ladybug flitted by my ear and I ducked. In the

distance, I heard lowing, as if somewhere in this massive space we could find other animals as well. I looked back to see if my friends had their mouths open in awe, too. Howard was digging with his toe in the dirt to see how deep it went. Eric was hopping from buttressed root to buttressed root, testing out his half-g powers.

Savannah hopped up next to me. "Wow."

I leaned into her, relieved that someone else realized how wild this was. "Yeah."

"I mean . . . he kills all those bees . . . and then he makes this?" She shrugged. Now that gravity was working on us again, wisps of her hair that had escaped its ponytail hung down in straggles around her face, and she swiped them away from her eyes with the back of her hand. "I don't like him at all, but this is impressive." She turned and called to Anton. "Is this what happens to your Eureka Cove flocks and colonies after their 'completion dates' on the island?"

Anton nodded. At least he didn't kill them, like we'd thought.

"We're trying to make life sustainable in space. This is merely the first step. We have to see how these species do long-term in confined spaces and under lower gravitational forces than they are used to. Eureka Cove was the first stage. This is stage two."

"It's amazing!" said Eric. "It's like a whole forest!"

Nate bounced lightly on his toes. "I told you this place

was amazing. Scary . . . but really awesome, too."

Anton gazed out over the woods, beaming with pride. "There are fields on the other side, for the farm animals. We can walk down there and see them if you like."

I looked at him. This was the Anton I'd met at dinner the other night, passionately arguing for the future of the human race. Somehow I'd forgotten that after seeing his warehouse of dead bees and knowing that he'd set out to terrorize people. I still didn't agree with his tactics. I never would. But somehow, I understood where he was coming from, now that I saw the end goal.

"Has Dani seen this?" I asked.

"She hasn't been up here since we got this new ring complete," he said, then frowned. "Actually, she hasn't come up at all since soon after the rediscovery of Omega City. I suppose it was because she was too busy sabotaging everything we were doing for the benefit of her *father*."

I didn't like the way his tone had turned bitter and mocking.

"Was she allowed?" I asked.

"Of course!" he snapped. "Dani was a senior Shepherd official. She didn't need anyone's permission to come—" He stopped, probably remembering how Dani wasn't even allowed in Omega City.

"You knew Dr. Underberg was sneaking onto this station," I said. "And Elana was doing everything in her power to keep Dani away from him. Maybe she hasn't been up here for a year because Elana wouldn't let her."

Anton looked pensive. "Dani never said anything. I just thought she'd lost interest . . ." He turned away, looking out into the forest.

"I bet she would have really liked this," Savannah said to him.

His eyes didn't lose their faraway glaze, but a hint of a smile crossed his features. "Probably. She always said she never saw a future for us. But this"—he spread his hands—"this is the future I see."

I stared out at the habitat. Was this where humanity was headed? Giant wheels in space, spreading outward forever?

"Why would Elana want to ruin this?" I asked. "She's a Shepherd. Isn't this the whole point of being a Shepherd?"

I hated the Shepherds and I'd never dream of laying a finger on Infinity Base. It was like Omega City itself, a testament to the will of human achievement. This wasn't a couple of astronauts floating around inside a glorified tin can. This was *life. In space.*

Anton whirled on me. "What are you talking about?"

I folded my hands defensively. "That's what she said, back on the ground. That she couldn't let Dr. Underberg's data get out, no matter what, even if it cost her Infinity Base."

She'd said it twice, in fact. Once when we were still underground, hiding outside the biostation while Elana and Dani loaded my unconscious father into a hypothermic torpor pod, and again on the phone, when she thought I was Dani and she was launching my dad into space.

He narrowed his eyes for a moment, as if trying to parse my words, then shook his head. "You must have misunderstood her. Elana has spent years on this project. It's our group's crowning achievement. Everything she does for Guidant is so we have the funds to make this possible. The smart courts, her consumer tracking software—"

"Right," I said. "The ones that invade our privacy and keep tabs on anything we've ever bought."

"It'll make a billion dollars," said Anton. "Each of these rings cost a billion dollars. Space isn't cheap, but everything we do, we do for humanity's future."

Elana had said that, too, on the phone. Guidant Technology had paid for Infinity Base. And by protecting Guidant, she could pay for a hundred space stations. But if Dr. Underberg released his data on Guidant's program hacks, the company would be ruined, and the Shepherds would lose all their income.

I wondered if I should tell Anton that. If I were really a Shepherd—really believed all the things Shepherds had been taught to believe, like Anton and Dani had their whole lives—what would I want?

On one hand, Anton clearly loved this station. And as strange as he was, I had to agree with him on that. I'd never seen anything like Infinity Base. Omega City had been awe-inspiring, but this place was literally out of this world. I couldn't imagine that he'd ever want to let it get destroyed.

On the other hand, Shepherds were weird. Anton shrugged off killing millions of bees. He didn't seem to understand why Dani would want to protect her own father. They lied to the whole world and destroyed people's lives and kidnapped entire families to get what they wanted and it didn't bother them. If Elana could just make him another space station, maybe he wouldn't actually care if this one was destroyed.

I wasn't sure which answer was right, or which one would be playing the game the way we were supposed to. This was probably the type of thing Dad would be better at figuring out.

"How many animals are there in this ring?" Savannah asked, probably to fill the awkward silence.

"I actually have an exact number," said Anton. He turned to a panel set in the wall and pressed a button, opening it up to reveal a double row of machines.

"Robots!" Eric exclaimed. He hopped down from the root he'd been standing on and bounded over with long leaps.

The ones on the top were flying drones, like the machines we'd seen feeding the sheep at Eureka Cove. The ones on the bottom had six legs and looked more like cat-size tarantulas. As they came online, each detached itself from its charging bay on the wall and fanned out across the space. I ducked when the flying drones buzzed over my head and hopped up on a branch as the spidery ones skittered past me on their way into the forest.

Eric took one look at the spider ones and jumped onto a low tree branch. I didn't blame him.

"This is a recent project I was really proud of. Each of these drones has specialized programming to care for one species or one creature, depending. They work a bit like a tracking dog. You feed the drone a bit of the animal's DNA, and it will follow it inside the habitat. It's an excellent way to keep tabs on the animal—the drone will bring food or medicine as needed, and report back data on its habits or any special needs it might have. We have these guys all over the place, watering plants, checking on the silkworms, all the day-to-day tasks. It helps keep our staff requirements low."

"Wow," said Savannah, watching the robots flit here and there among the wildlife. "It's nice to know you don't just want to kill animals."

Anton ignored that. "What I wanted to do was give this technology to wildlife conservationists back home.

Imagine if you could track each individual member of an endangered species with a drone. I was especially keen on getting drone protection for species endangered due to poaching, like tigers and rhinos."

"That's great!" said Savannah. "Why haven't you?"

"I will," he insisted. "It's just . . . it's a very expensive project, and there are more immediate commercial uses for the technology at present."

"Like what?" she asked.

"Like the military," Nate said. We looked at him and he shrugged and hopped clear over a tree root nearly as tall as he was. "I'm right, aren't I?"

"Yes." Anton did not sound happy about it.

"Ha!" Nate sounded triumphant. "Take that, brain damage!"

"How did you know?" I asked him.

"Because that's how it works," Howard answered for him. "That's how it always works. Scientists invent things, and the military uses it first. Worked with the space program, works with the Shepherds."

"We already have drones in the military," I said.

"Yes, but imagine you could train a drone to only shoot people with certain DNA markers," said Anton. "You could even feed it the DNA of a terrorist and have the drone root them out. Like a robot assassin."

I went cold all over. "So then all you would need to

target someone is to feed it a bit of their DNA?"

Those spidery drones had just gone from vaguely creepy to absolutely terrifying. And the ones flitting about my head were even worse.

"Don't worry, don't worry!" Anton called, laughing as I ducked as one buzzed my head. "It's not like they have guns or anything on them. These are just feeding drones. The worst they can do is drop pellets on you or mist you with antibacterial spray."

One of the spider drones skittered close to Eric, who punted it into the far wall.

"Hey!" Anton said sharply. "I just finished telling you how expensive they are!"

"What is it with this guy and bugs?" Eric asked.

"These are robots," said Anton.

Yeah, scary robots that wanted our DNA so they could target us. Creepy. "Can you put them away?" I liked the forest, but I could do without the killer robots from outer space.

Anton rolled his eyes, then turned to the panel in the wall, and all the drones zipped and skittered back into their little pen. "I never understood why people think animals are so cute, but robots are so creepy."

"I don't think all your robots are creepy," Eric said helpfully. "I really liked the waiter at the restaurant that time." He looked at me and shrugged helplessly.

Well, Dad said we didn't have to be perfect supporters of every single Shepherd project. And tarantula robots were a perfectly natural thing to fear.

Still, the forest was beautiful. We wandered the full length of the ring, enjoying both the feel of up and down, however slight, and the pretty plants and miniature animals. Alongside the sheep and goats were bunnies, birds, and even lizards. I felt light, and not just because I weighed less than fifty pounds. It was easy to pretend to like the Shepherds in this outer-space park. I wasn't sure I was even pretending, after a while.

Anton looked down at his wrist, where his digital watch face buzzed and beeped. "That's odd," he said. "I'm getting a call from the main chamber. Maybe Dr. Underberg has woken up again."

He pressed a button on the side of the face. "Hello?"

"Anton." It was a woman's voice. Elana's voice.

I stumbled on my next step and tumbled head over heels into the undergrowth.

"Elana?" Anton's voice cracked on the words. "What are you doing here? How did you get up here?"

"I took the second shuttle the moment I realized what Dani and those children were up to."

"You—you should have told me you were coming—"

"Why? Would it have stopped you from betraying me?"

"*Betraying* you!" He gasped. "We had a plan, yes,

but I've been talking with our guests, and I think there's a way—"

"First Dani, now you. And you wonder why I'm here myself?" She sounded more annoyed than truly angry. I recalled what Dani had said about Elana back at the bio-station. *You don't get to be the leader of the Shepherds and the head of a multibillion-dollar tech company without making sure that the people who work for you are obeying your orders.*

"Elana, what are you doing?" Anton asked.

"I'm taking care of our problem," she replied. "Once and for all."

NOTHING BUT THE TRUTH

I DIDN'T WAIT TO HEAR THE REST OF THE CONVERSATION. ELANA MERO was up in the stem of the space station with Dad and Dr. Underberg, and she was very, very angry. I took off, my strides more like jumps as I weaved through the forest back to the entrance to the spoke tunnel. The others followed behind me.

"Come on!" I started up the ladder, taking the rungs two at a time. The lack of gravity helped as I leaped up rung after rung. I felt like a jungle cat . . . at least, until I was two-thirds of the way to the top, where the gravity grew low and I was passed by Eric, who was actually running on his hands and feet up the side of the wall.

"Go, go!" Nate shouted from behind me. I was barely using the rungs now, just a touch here and there to push myself higher as I reached the weightlessness of free-fall.

Up ahead, I saw Eric slide through the hatch door. The window was closing. I dove in, flying into the wall in the corridor on the other side. I turned around and looked back, but the lights had gone red and the hatch was closed. I saw Anton's face as it rotated out of sight. We had forty seconds until it opened again, but not a moment to waste.

"They'll follow us," Eric assured me, and took off down the hall toward the back end of the station. I pushed off and flew after him, kicking and pushing off the walls to propel me through the chambers. Eric glided through the air like some strange bird, shooting through small hatches with perfect aim while I struggled to angle my body right, crashing and bumping into edges.

Behind me, I could hear Anton, Howard, Nate, and Savannah bursting out of the tunnel when it reopened, but I concentrated on moving. I had no idea what we'd find when we got there. Elana, maybe, or a whole host of Shepherds.

But it was something even worse. An alarm sounded somewhere, and with it, a recorded announcement.

Warning. Fire detected on adjoined spacecraft. Danger from artificial atmosphere contamination. Air lock closed.

"They're locked out!" I cried.

At last we flew through the final portal into the last chamber, the one with the air lock to *Knowledge*. Indeed, the air-lock door was shut tight, and Elana Mero hovered in front of it, frowning furiously.

"What did you do!" my brother bellowed, and launched himself at her. She spun in the air and caught him, twisting his arms up behind his back. Eric cried out in pain.

I wasn't sure what to do. How could I pull him away from her with nothing to grab on to?

"Let go of me!" my brother screamed. He yanked his knees up to his chest and kicked out at her, catching her arm and her face. Elana yelped as her grip on his arm slipped. Eric shot back toward me and we collided against the wall near the entrance door.

"Eric!" I sighed with relief and wrapped my arms tight around my brother. Elana rolled off the wall, rubbing her jaw.

"She's quick," he warned me. "Quicker than Dani."

"Elana!" Anton's voice boomed as his large form sailed through the door into the chamber. "Stop!"

She spun to face him and her hair followed, the usually sleek bob floating up around her face like a sharp black halo. "What in the world do you think you're doing up here?" she raged at him. "You had strict orders—"

"No one gives me strict orders on Infinity Base," he

snapped back. "You may call the shots at Guidant, but this is my territory. And I thought it was worth another try."

Warning. Fire detected on adjoined spacecraft. Danger from artificial atmosphere contamination. Air lock closed.

"What is this?" Anton pushed past her to tug at the air-lock door.

"It was supposed to be a small, controlled explosion. But clearly I can't count on anything working the way it's supposed to, can I?" Her expression was one of bored frustration, as if she were having trouble with her phone instead of an explosion. "The fire will probably do the trick, though."

"Dad!" I sobbed.

Anton rushed to a screen and started jabbing at it furiously. "Maybe he's unblocked the closed-circuit video. There!"

The view of Dr. Underberg's command terminal appeared. There was fire burning in the background, and smoke hung thick in the air. Dr. Underberg was slumped forward in his chair and my father was floating beside him. His face was blackened and smeared with blood.

"Dad!" Eric shouted. "You're alive."

Dad startled at the noise, then looked around. "Eric? Where are you?"

We waved our arms. "On the screen!"

"The screen's on fire," he said, then coughed heavily. "Everything is on fire."

"Dr. Seagret." Howard pushed past me. "There's a fire extinguisher right next to the command terminal. You have to put it out before the artificial atmosphere causes an explosion. Do you see it? All you have to do is pull down and aim. The trigger will release like shooting a gun."

I sighed with relief. At least someone here knew how Underberg's spaceship worked.

Dad coughed again, but felt around on the terminal to pull the extinguisher free.

"There's a lot of smoke," he said, over the sound of the extinguisher. "I don't know if I can get it all."

I hurried back to the air lock. "Open this door!" I shouted to Anton. "I have to get my father!"

"It won't open," Anton said. "The fire might cause an explosion and destroy the base." He whirled on Elana. "What are you going to do, kill all of them?"

Elana snorted in disdain. "These people will never understand us, and these children have been far more trouble than they are worth."

"They brought us Omega City," Anton replied.

"And they unleashed Dr. Underberg on us. Before, he was contained, a little old man, buried underground. Now he has what he needs to destroy everything we've built. Anton, if his information gets out, it will be the end of Guidant. The end of everything we've worked for."

"And if we don't have another generation of Shepherds, we'll be at an end, too," said Anton.

"You sound like Dani," Elana scoffed. "What's next, babies? I thought you'd decided against all that non-sense."

"Just because I don't want to add to overpopulation on the planet doesn't mean I don't think we need to recruit. And these kids are smart."

"Oh, I know they are smart. They're smarter than you. You think you have them convinced, or are they just biding their time until they're out of *your territory?*"

I breathed in sharply and hugged Eric as tightly as I could.

"You were supposed to get rid of them," Elana said, "not play tour guide."

"And *you* were supposed to make sure that they were in the pods," Anton fired back. "I guess we both made errors."

"Dani tricked me," cried Elana. "She's been tricking us all, for months. She's been helping Underberg!"

Warning. Fire detected on adjoined spacecraft. Danger from artificial atmosphere contamination. Air lock closed.

They were having a debate while my father fought for his life.

"Please!" I begged Anton. "Please, you have to tell us how to open the door."

He looked at me sadly. "It can't be opened." Then he turned back to Elana. "And, on that topic, what is this about you not letting Dani into Omega City?"

What did any of that matter now?

"*HELP US!*" I shouted at the top of my lungs.

They both looked at me. Elana tsked. "Little girl, the grown-ups are talking." She shook her head, as if appalled by my behavior. I was pretty appalled by hers.

I'd known for years that the Shepherds didn't care whose lives they ruined to get their way, but now I was floating here watching it happen. To me.

"You can't imagine that I'll let this stand," Anton said.

But she just shrugged. "I think the organization is going to side with me. Sorry, Anton. It would be a pity to lose you, but the Shepherds have survived the defection of greater minds than yours." She gestured through the air lock toward *Knowledge* and I shook with rage. That was my father in there.

Anton looked pretty angry himself. "You might have killed all of us. You might have destroyed this base."

"Don't be dramatic. You're as bad as these kids."

Nothing seemed to bother her. It was all a game. She would win and everyone else would lose, as long as the rules worked in her favor. It was like Dani had said back on Earth—Shepherds had their own rules of right and wrong, and it colored everything they did. Good and bad, dead and alive, us and Them.

If you weren't with the Shepherds, you were against Them. And that meant you had to be destroyed. Suddenly, it hit me.

Dani had been misinformed. There *was* a difference between truth and lies. There *was* such a thing as right and wrong, even for the Shepherds. And I was staring right at it.

"Elana doesn't care about Infinity Base." My voice was cold and bright as a bell. "She doesn't care about the Shepherds or their dream of the stars. All she cares about is her own power. She'll destroy everything you've built if given the chance."

Anton hadn't believed me, back in the centrifuge ring. I had to make him believe me this time. It was harder to dismiss it now that she was here and setting spaceships on fire.

I pointed an accusing finger at the head of Guidant

Technologies. "She said she would. Back on the ground. She said she'd do what she had to, to make sure Guidant was safe, that her secrets were safe. Even if it meant killing us. Even if it meant destroying Infinity Base. And now she's here to do it."

Anton grew very stiff, his large, gangly form stretching from one side of the room to the other. He turned his head toward Elana. "You didn't say that."

"I certainly didn't say it to *her*. She's nothing."

It was an answer designed for a Shepherd, but Anton wasn't buying it. "But . . . you wouldn't say it."

Elana sighed and shut her eyes for a moment. "I can't believe I have to explain this again. This base costs money. Lots of money, that Guidant is responsible for. Guidant is our future."

"*Infinity Base* is our future." If he could have stamped the ground he stood on, he would have.

Elana rubbed her temples with bone-deep weariness. "Do you have any idea how delusional you sound?"

Her words fell like a slap. I don't know if she even realized it. Anton's face was a mottled mask of confusion and fury. I was so close.

Us. And Them.

"See?" I said. "She doesn't care about the Shepherd mission or the future of the human race. Not like Dr. Underberg. Not like my dad." I stumbled over the last word as I thought of my father, trapped on the spaceship. But freaking out wasn't going to help. It was just like when he told us to pretend to be Shepherds. We had to convince Anton that we were the ones on his team.

Except this time, we actually were.

The undeniable truth of my words was washing over Anton. Elana saw it, and her expression changed. "That's not so," she said quickly. "I've poured billions into this station—"

"She buried Omega City." I kept going. "She tried to ruin my father—"

"Shut up," she said dangerously, looking angry for the first time. As angry as she'd been back at the biostation when she kidnapped Dad and Nate.

It was working. "She doesn't care about anything but her tech company," I insisted. "And if you let her, she'll destroy everything you've built, just like she did to Underberg."

"Anton." Elana's voice dripped with sarcasm. "You can't be listening to this. It's ridiculous. After all the money I've given you for your little projects?"

"My little *delusional* projects?" Anton shot back. "And what about Dani? "You've cut her out of everything—"

"With good reason!" Elana exclaimed. "She's been sabotaging us. She obviously couldn't be trusted."

I took a deep, shuddering breath. I could do this. I

could. "Dani's probably dead. And if you let Elana get away with this, we'll all be next."

Elana shot toward me, arms outstretched. "You don't know what you're talking about, you stupid little girl—"

Out of nowhere, two flashes of silver slammed into her.

"Leave my sister alone!" Eric cried as he and Savannah shoved her across the chamber. Nate came flying after them.

"Guys!" he shouted. "Guys, settle down."

Elana started shrieking and kicking.

"Okay, then," he amended. "Let me help."

Anton's face was set in hard lines and he moved to one of the cabinets. "Elana," he said grimly, "you've become a danger to yourself and others on this station." He pulled a packet out of a cabinet and crossed over to where Elana was struggling to pull herself free from the three kids holding her. "I have no choice but to stop you."

I recognized the tranquilizer dart in his hand. I guess he and Dani did have a lot in common. He stuck the needle into Elana's neck. She struggled for a few moments more, then slumped. Her dark bob floated over her face.

Anton stood over her, shaking his head. "I really, really hate doing that."

In that moment, I believed it. Anton might be crazy, but he had never once been violent. He'd killed a lot of bees, but he really did seem to want to save the human race.

And maybe he could still save Dad.

Warning. Fire detected on adjoined spacecraft. Emergency detachment imminent.

Detachment? Like they were going to cut the spaceship loose? "Stop!" I screamed. I ran back to the screen.

Howard was still at the microphone, speaking as calmly to my father as if he'd trained his entire life for this moment. He might not even have noticed the commotion going on around him. "Dr. Seagret, put down the extinguisher. You need to engage your life-support systems. Find a helmet."

On-screen, Dr. Underberg groaned and shifted. I saw him say something to my father, but couldn't make out what it was. Dad looked up and around.

"What's a PRE?" he asked the sky.

Howard jumped back in. "It's a personal rescue enclosure. I didn't know they were ever used. It's like a bubble made of space suit material for emergency abandon-ship scenarios. Maybe there's one near the hatch. . . ."

The screen went dark.

"Get them back!" Eric shouted. "Get them back!"

Warning. Fire detected on adjoined spacecraft. Emergency detachment in progress.

There was a horrific clunking sound from the docking port, and then a mechanical whirring.

"Stop!" I cried at the machinery. "You can't detach them!"

I lunged at the air lock, as if it would do any good. Savannah sobbed.

Howard was still listing instructions for my father. I had no idea if he could hear any of them.

At the other end of the air lock, I thought I saw movement. For a second, I thought it might be Dad, making it through, but then the window fogged up and I realized it was Underberg's ships moving away.

I couldn't even scream.

The others were shouting around me, though.

"Nate," said Anton, and his voice was as even-keeled as Howard's has been. "Help me get in my EVA."

"What's that?" he asked, frantic.

"His space suit," said Howard. "Help him get into his space suit."

How were they so calm? How could they be so calm? I tried to remember that Anton had trained for this. Like a real astronaut. And Howard—well, he'd practically

271

trained. In his head, anyway.

Eric grabbed on to me, and so did Savannah. "Where are they?" he whispered.

Howard stood at the screen and pulled up another view, this one external. I could see the tail end of Infinity Base, and beyond it, the hulking, misshapen mass of the conjoined *Wisdom* and *Knowledge*, floating a few yards away. From here, they didn't even look like they were on fire. And maybe they weren't. After all, a fire needed oxygen. Just like Dad and Dr. Underberg.

"Look!" Howard exclaimed, pointing at the screen where *Knowledge* and *Wisdom* were floating ever farther away. I couldn't look. I couldn't.

"Gillian," Howard said softly, and wonder of wonders, I felt his hand touch mine. I looked up at his face, and he was looking in my eyes. I'd forgotten how pretty his eyes were, since he never looked at me. Like Nate's. A moment passed, and I realized I was breathing again.

He turned back to the screen and pointed. There, bobbing right at the edge of the camera's view, was a tiny white-and-silver ball. "He must have deployed it."

Hope fluttered in my chest. "Is he inside?"

Howard squinted at the image, looking for the clear panel that would reveal the contents of the ball. "I think . . . I see a head?"

Dad! I breathed a huge sigh of relief.

"How long can he last in there?" Eric asked.

"They are supposed to come equipped with an hour of oxygen," said Howard. "I don't know, though. They were never used. And they only fit one person."

My eyes began to burn. So Dr. Underberg was going down with his ship.

Nate was busy strapping Anton into a space suit. I expected Howard to help, too, but he just floated there with me, holding my hand as we stared at that tiny silver bubble bobbing alone in space.

Anton put on his helmet, then eased his way through the hatch and into the air lock, closing the inner door behind him. We watched through the porthole as he attached himself to a life-support backpack, a giant mobility unit, and a retractable cord fastened to the station itself.

"Anton Everett" came a voice over the speaker.

"All clear for rescue mission," Anton said, then leaned over and opened the outer air lock door.

He was whooshed into space like a leaf down a river and I turned back to the screen, watching his even tinier form spool out over the horizon.

"Deploying thrusters thirty degrees, about fourteen meters from target." I thought his voice would sound tinny, like Neil Armstrong did on the moon, but it sounded like he was talking to us over the phone. "Five meters and closing."

The tiny figure met with the ball.

"Target secured. Retracting cord now."

I started crying for real now, and all five of us fell into one big hug. "We got him, we got him."

And Dr. Underberg was really, really gone.

Within a few minutes, Anton had returned to the station and managed to maneuver himself and the ball inside the air lock. They were so crowded in there I couldn't see the clear panel that would have showed my father inside. The air lock closed and pressurized, and we were able to open the hatch. Anton worked his way past the ball and into the port cabin, and as soon as he was through, Eric and I scrambled back over into the air lock and started pulling at the zippers and sealed locks.

"Did it stay pressurized?" Anton asked, climbing back into the room. He had a medical kit in his hands.

The ball cracked open like a hard-boiled egg and my dad slumped out, an oxygen mask dangling haphazardly over the side of his face. He smelled smoky, even through my stuffed nose. I leaned in to press my ear to his chest, then noticed he was a lot lumpier inside the ball than I was expecting. I shifted the thick material around as well as I could in the microgravity.

Dr. Underberg flopped out, and I shot to my feet, banging into the far wall.

"Out of the way!" Anton yelled, and Eric and I backed

up as Anton shoved an oxygen mask on the old man. "Get your father back inside."

Thankfully, he was weightless. Eric and I struggled to maneuver him through the air lock on our own, but once we got him halfway in, Nate and Savannah helped us pull him inside. Howard came over with another oxygen mask and helped secure it over his mouth and behind his head, while Nate held him against the wall and got a belt to secure him so he wouldn't float all over and could rest.

"Dad, can you hear me?" I hovered over him, holding his face in my hands.

He coughed and looked at me with bleary eyes. "Can we go home now?"

FATHERS AND DAUGHTERS

DR. UNDERBERG WAS ALIVE. BARELY.

In order to deal with their depressurization and reduce the need for constant oxygen and continual monitoring on the station, Anton had placed both Dr. Underberg and my father back in hypothermic torpor. He did the same for Elana, too, in order to, as he put it, get her out of the way.

He also tried to talk the rest of us into it.

"Honestly, it'll make for a more pleasant trip home," he said.

"Forget it," said Nate, crossing his arms.

"Yeah!" said Howard, copying his brother's stance. "I want to see what it's like to reenter the Earth's atmosphere."

We all stared at him.

"What?" he asked. "Is that not why?"

"No," Nate said. "That's not why. The why is we're not getting knocked out and shoved in a box. Been there, done that. I'm going to be in control of what happens to my body from now on."

"Oh," said Howard. "Yeah, that, too." He crossed his arms again.

Anton scoffed at that. "Kid, how in control do you think you are when landing a spacecraft? I'm a trained pilot and I depend almost entirely on the computers and ground control."

"Ground control?" I said. "Wait, you mean the people landing us are Shepherds?"

Anton spread his arms. "This entire operation is Shepherds, remember? Secret space station?"

Right. That. I guess it was time to talk about that. I floated over to the porthole and looked out at space. I'd saved Dad and Dr. Underberg. I'd even convinced Anton to take us back home. But we still had to deal with the Shepherds.

I looked at Anton. He was so creepy, so terrifying. But he'd saved my father's life. He'd had those tranquilizers on him the whole time, but instead he'd chosen to talk to us, to try to convince us of the power of his mission. He'd killed a bunch of bees, but he wanted to save the world.

I thought of home, and our silly cat, Paper Clip, and the way that people throughout history had done bad things for the good of all mankind. Even when we knew the truth, it didn't diminish what had been accomplished. The lies were a tarnish on the fabric of history, but we still fought to move forward. To make progress, like Dr. Underberg dreamed.

Despite all their lies and manipulations, the Shepherds had created something extraordinary in Infinity Base, just as they had created something extraordinary in Omega City. I didn't want to see it shut down. I wanted a way for it to remain, for the good of all humanity. Like the Shepherds once thought, back when Dr. Underberg had been young and full of hope for the future.

"I want people to know the truth," I said. "The truth about what you've managed to accomplish here. Infinity Base is only a secret because that's the way the Shepherds want to operate. But isn't it the Shepherds who have lost their way?"

Eric whistled. "Gills, you've gone to the dark side. Really. You're lucky Dad's frozen."

I looked at him. "No, this is exactly what Dad wrote about. Dr. Underberg left the Shepherds when they tried to keep Omega City to themselves. And now they're doing it again."

Savannah nodded vigorously. "You think letting us go,

letting your secrets be exposed means you're turning on the Shepherds. But it's really the Shepherds who were turning on their mission. You say you want to help humanity, but look at all the ways you've hurt people. And . . . bees."

I kept going. "People deserved to know about Omega City, and everyone on Earth deserves to know about what you've created up here."

Anton's brows were furrowed. He was raised a Shepherd, just like Dani. They were steeped in secrecy and self-importance, but there was one part of their beliefs that trumped all. Everything they were doing was supposed to be for the good of mankind, to help humanity survive the future.

"We'll all get arrested," he said after a minute of thought.

"Good," murmured Nate.

Savannah gave him a dirty look, then looked back at Anton. "You might," she agreed. "For, like, kidnapping. And fraud."

"And conspiracy," Eric added. "This is definitely a clear case of conspiracy. Even I can see that."

"But you also stopped an even bigger conspiracy. You could be the whistle-blower. Maybe you get immunity for that."

"Or time off for the good behavior of building a really awesome space station and gifting it to the world,"

I finished. "This place—Infinity Base—Anton, it's the future. Don't you think the world should claim it?"

FOR THE RECORD, spacecraft landings are . . . boring. It took us ten heart-pounding minutes to get into space. It took us about six uneventful, turbulent hours in a Shepherd shuttle covered completely with heat shields to make it back to Earth. Eric complained that they should have in-flight video games. Nate, I'm pretty sure, took a nap somewhere above China. Howard read every single line of data, from altimeter and velocity readings to heat and life-support checks.

I kept my screen trained on the cargo area, where the three hypothermic transport pods containing Elana, Dad, and Dr. Underberg were strapped in tight.

I had no idea what awaited us on the ground. Anton had been in several intense conversations with Shepherd personnel back home, and we'd even gotten the chance to have a short chat with Dani and my mother, in order to assure us that we weren't walking into another Shepherd trap. They'd both been released, and from what I could see, Dani was back in charge of operations.

I was hoping that was a good thing.

Anton had decided to stay aboard the station. I was pretty sure it was his way of avoiding arrest, at least for a little while.

"I'm not going back," he'd said to us, his eyes firmly trained on one of Infinity Base's many checklist screens. "Whatever happens, the continuation of Infinity Base is now in question. Without Guidant resources, I don't know what will keep this station going. No new research, no new supplies. . . . You've seen the things I have up here," he said. "The ecosystem I've created. I can't abandon them."

"You can't *stay* here," said Savannah. "Alone?"

"Dr. Underberg did," Anton said. "He was in that spaceship for nearly a year."

"And look what happened to him!" Eric said.

"Infinity Base has much better resources," Anton said. "Astronauts stay in the International Space Station for months at a time and they don't have nearly the radiation shielding or the benefits of artificial gravity sections that I will here."

"They also have support from multiple countries and private corporations," Howard pointed out.

"Hopefully, that will be the deal the Shepherds work out with the international community," said Anton. "But I'm not going to risk losing my station while we wait to find out."

I watched him working the screens as if he hadn't a care in the world, and realized another clarion truth. "You want to go down with the ship."

281

Like Dr. Underberg. These Shepherds. Their priorities were all screwed up.

For a moment, there was nothing but the sounds of machinery and artificial atmosphere. You could have heard a pin drop, if pins dropped in zero g.

"What I want, Miss Seagret," said Anton, "is for the *ship* not to go down, And I feel like my best protection against such an eventuality is to not abandon it here."

I'd run out of energy to argue, and when I looked at the others, they didn't seem to think it was worth it, either. If Dr. Underberg could survive for months on a broken-down rocket from the eighties, maybe Anton would be okay up here.

So we'd left without him. And endured six hours with no communication from the ground or Infinity Base.

"This would be cooler," said Howard, "if we could see the part where we catch fire."

"Yeah," said Savannah sarcastically. "That's *just* what this trip is missing."

Eric harrumphed in agreement.

THERE WAS A moment of excitement when the parachutes deployed and we began, at last, to really slow down. We all jerked in our seats at the sudden deceleration, and I held my breath for a moment, terrified that something had gone wrong and we were about to crash.

We didn't. Instead we started a long, slow drift to the ground. Very long. Very slow. Nate fell asleep again.

Two hours later, we touched down, as planned, on the Shepherds' landing field. And there we sat, for another hour or so, until someone came to pry us out of our capsule.

There was a mechanical sound on the hatch, as whatever locks were applied to the door were pried loose, and then a line of daylight, real daylight. I craned my neck to watch as the door was removed, and then a figure appeared, shadowed by the sunshine behind her.

"You all are grounded," said my mother. "Permanently."

"Mom!" cried Eric, fumbling for his seat belt. I quickly unhooked mine and then tried to stand up in my seat, only to stumble and fall as the full weight of the Earth hit me again.

"Watch out," she said, and pulled me up and into a hug. "Gravity will kill you."

Actually, it was my brother who would, as Eric barreled me down again as he climbed over me and into my mother's arms. Our helmets knocked together.

"Mom! Mom! You're all right," he cried, his voice muffled by his helmet.

"I'm thrilled to see you, too," she said.

Behind her, I saw the field was swarming with cops. *Real* cops. There were men and women in jackets emblazoned with the letters "FBI" holding back what had to be dozens of reporters with big microphones and even bigger cameras. I saw vans with satellites on their roofs, and helicopters circling overhead.

I guess it wasn't every day you learned about the existence of a secret space station.

More personnel were coming in. I'd expected to see Shepherd or Guidant uniforms, but these staffers were wearing orange outfits with the NASA logo.

"Are they getting Dad?" I asked. "And Dr. Underberg? They need medical attention."

"Like it or not, you're all headed to the hospital."

Mom was right. We were herded straight into the back of an ambulance and all went to some kind of military hospital. There were guards at the door. No TV in the rooms. There were people in dark suits standing in the hall, and no one got in except for the nurses and doctors on duty, the Nolands, and Savannah's mother.

Mrs. Noland looked like she'd aged about ten years since I'd seen her at Howard's birthday party. Mr. Noland was quiet, but every few minutes, he found some reason to hug both the boys. Even Howard tolerated it.

Ms. Fairchild told Savannah she was fielding calls from film agents. The people in dark suits didn't seem to like the sound of that at all.

Meanwhile, the doctors took about ten vials of our

blood and evaluated our hearts and lungs for "deleterious effects of space travel on adolescent respiratory systems."

Apparently outer space is bad for your lungs. Who knew?

No one would tell us what happened to Dr. Underberg. No one would tell us what had happened to the Shepherds.

And even after they'd determined we were all just fine, they didn't let us go. Instead we were relegated to a drab waiting room, where decade-old issues of magazines sat alongside dusty, threadbare *Reader's Digest* collections. There were pictures of kittens and fairgrounds on the wall, and a Scrabble box missing—as Howard dutifully reported—two Ss, three Es, and a J.

He and Nate tried to play, anyway. Eric got super into some story in *Reader's Digest* about a dog. Savannah asked for some scissors, and spent her time making hexaflexagons. I climbed the walls.

"Sit down," Savannah said to me. She pushed some paper my way. "You're making me nervous."

"I don't know how you aren't nervous already," I replied. "We don't know if Dr. Underberg survived the trip. We don't know what was going on with the Shepherds and Elana. We don't know what's happening outside this room! Is the world finding out about Infinity Base?"

Savannah chuckled. "Are you worried someone is going to scoop your dad's next book?"

I laughed ruefully.

"You did it, Gillian," she said. "You saved your dad."

I sat down next to her. "*We* did," I corrected. "And I think we kind of saved the whole world, too."

"Yeah," agreed Savannah. "I think that's going to be really good for Nate's college essays."

"Not to mention your future film deal."

The two of us started laughing uncontrollably.

"Remember me when you get to Hollywood," I said.

"At least California is closer to Idaho," she replied.

That pretty much stopped the laughter. "I'm going to miss you next year."

"Yeah?" She folded the flexagon back and forth to crease the seams. "I'm starting to wonder if maybe it's a good thing you're going."

"Hey!" I said, indignant.

"When you only lived in town for the summers, I never once almost died. And now it happens all the time." She smirked. "I really don't have time for that. I need to focus on middle school."

"All those new boys?"

"All that precalculus."

I leaned my head on her shoulder. I'd still miss her. I'd miss all of them. Except Eric. He'd be right there with me, driving me nuts and saving my life. I grinned at him and he looked up from his book.

"Why are you staring at me?" he asked, sticking his tongue out.

"I love you."

"Uh-huh." He went back to his story, but I could see him smiling like a fool at the page.

Mom came in a few minutes later, looking worried but rested, with her hair freshly washed and a clean set of clothes on.

"Mom!" I cried, leaping up to give her a hug.

"Oof." She caught me, then squeezed me tight. "I could get used to this."

"Where is Dad? When are they letting us out of here? What's going on? What's happening with the Shepherds? With Infinity Base? What about Dr. Underberg?"

She smiled weakly. "Okay, settle down. Those are a lot of questions."

I blinked at her. "So?"

"Never change, kiddo," she said. "You really are your father's daughter."

As if there had been any doubt.

"Look, Gillian, it's complicated. I don't really understand all this stuff. National security, everything. This is your dad's area."

"Where's Dad?"

"Recovering," she said. "And I don't think even he would know where to begin with these people. We're all under a massive gag order. But from what she's told me, Dani has it under control."

"Dani?" Eric asked, looking up from his book. "You mean she's getting something right for a change?"

"Thanks for the vote of confidence." I looked over to the door to see Dani Alcestis standing there. She'd done her hair again—it was back to the perfect, sleek yellow swoop—and she was wearing a classy black suit and silk blouse. "It's always so lovely to do business with you Sea-grets."

I stood up. "You have to tell us what's going on!"

"So demanding," she said, wrinkling her nose. She strode into the room, taking in the decor. "And yes, trust me. I know I do. If I don't you'll just find a way to get the information anyway. Hey, nice hexaflexagon, Savannah."

Savannah held up her creation. "Thanks. This one has six faces, like the zipper pulls."

"Well done." She stood in the middle of the floor. "I'm glad to see you all have been keeping yourselves . . . busy."

Very funny. I tapped my foot. "What's happening with Infinity Base?"

"Nothing at the moment," she said. "You can't inform the governments of the world that you've built a secret space station and expect them to just take the keys and run. Any kind of transition at all is going to take a little time. At present, NASA and the CIA are just concerned we've built a massive orbiting death machine with missiles trained everywhere. They're busy making sure that's not the case."

"Oh, no!" cried Savannah. "They aren't going to do anything to hurt it, are they? Like, shoot it out of the sky or anything? There are all those animals up there."

"Indeed," said Dani lightly. "Plus Anton. But I doubt it. First of all, I don't think they could hit it with anything, even if they wanted to. The U.S. rocket program is a good decade behind ours. Secondly, they wouldn't destroy anything they could use. They just have to make themselves feel better by pretending to be careful and concerned. That's how governments work."

I rolled my eyes. Dani was back to smug Shepherd mode. I hadn't missed it. "Okay, so what about the Shepherds and Guidant?"

"Well, *I've* tendered my resignation at Guidant," Dani said. "It's funny. There have been a lot of resignations there over the past day or so. And a lot of arrests."

"So it's disconnected from the Shepherds," I clarified.

Dani looked at me blankly. "I really wouldn't know," she said, in a voice of innocence. "I have been busy with a family matter. My father has been very ill. Thanks for asking about him, by the way, Gillian. *Very* thoughtful."

"She is thoughtful," said Howard, from his Scrabble table. "Dr. Underberg isn't safe unless the Shepherds agree to leave him alone."

"Thanks, Howard." I turned back to Dani. "Leave all of us alone. *Are* the Shepherds doing what they promised?"

"*If* I had any knowledge of Shepherd activity, I would be inclined to say yes. I think whoever is in charge these days has Dr. Underberg's well-being as her utmost priority."

"Wait," said Howard. "Does that mean you—"

"Howard," I interrupted, because those guys with the suits were still listening. "I think she has it covered."

She smiled at me. I took a risk and smiled back.

Mom held out her hand. "Your father's awake," she said. "Do you want to see him?"

Eric and I went running.

DAD'S LUNGS HAD undergone some damage due to smoke inhalation during the fire on *Knowledge*, but otherwise he was in good shape. He was on antibiotics to keep infection from setting in, and still had the IV tube in his arm when Eric and I piled on his hospital bed.

"How's Dr. Underberg?" he asked, his voice crackly and wheezing.

"He's in the ICU," Dani said. She'd accompanied us to Dad's room. "His body has deteriorated quite a bit from his year in microgravity. Not just his bones and muscles, but his heart, his circulation, his lungs . . ." She swallowed. "They still aren't sure if he's going to make it back here on

Earth. He's almost ninety, you know."

"I'm so sorry, Dani," said my father. "I want you to know what an honor it was to spend time with him—"

"And I want to thank you, Dr. Seagret, for saving his life. I heard about what happened during the fire on his ship. That was incredibly quick thinking."

"You can thank Howard," said Dad. "He told me where to find the fire extinguisher and the rescue device. Everything was burning up, but Howard just kept talking."

Dani smiled. "Yes, I think we've got to keep our eye on that boy."

"I don't think he's seen the last of outer space," said Mom.

"I want to go back, too," said Eric. "It was cooler than swimming."

"Wow," said Dad. "High praise coming from you. What about you, Gillian? Are you going to be an astronaut now?"

I thought about it. I'd been terrified during liftoff, but the sight of the Earth from space was one I'd never forget. "I don't know," I admitted. "Maybe. I guess it depends what kind of future Infinity Base has to offer."

"Good answer," said Dani.

"Well, I'm done," Dad said. "I'll just have to watch you guys go."

I frowned. He would, wouldn't he? And not just to

space, either. We'd be going off to Idaho soon, with Mom. My thoughts must have been showing on my face, because Dad squeezed my hand, and I felt a sob rise in my throat.

"Not forever, kiddo!" he said to me. "Not forever. If there's one thing I learned on Infinity Base, it's that it doesn't matter how far away we are from each other. You and Eric and me—we'll always be a team." He reached out and hugged me. Eric came in, too.

A nurse appeared at the door.

"Miss Alcestis?" she said. "The patient is waking up. He'll want to see a familiar face."

Dani frowned. "I'm not . . . I'm not familiar."

The nurse faltered. "You don't want him to be alone right now . . ."

She looked at me. "Could the children . . . he knows the Seagrets better than me."

"It's not standard to allow children in the ICU. Certainly not five of them . . ."

And yet ten minutes later, there we were, surrounding the bed of Dr. Underberg. He looked even smaller here than he had in his ship, his wasted body and brittle skin almost as pale as the bedsheet. There were tubes and wires in his arm, his nose, and traveling under the bed. The skin around his face was shrunken to his skull. But the machines showed a steady heartbeat, and his chest rose and fell. There were seven of us there in the room: Nate and Howard, Savannah and Eric, Dad and Dani, and me.

On the monitors, his rate of respiration rose. His heartbeat quickened. His eyelashes fluttered. He opened his eyes and looked at us all, surrounding his bedside.

"Seagrets . . . ," he wheezed. "Where are we?"

"Back on Earth," said Howard, almost disappointed.

"Ah . . ." Dr. Underberg echoed the sentiment. He took us in one by one, then frowned. "I . . ."

I looked around. Dani was shying back, and I pulled her forward. "Dr. Underberg, allow me to introduce you to your daughter. This is Dani Alcestis."

"Hello." She tripped over the word and focused on the bedsheets, the floor, anything but her father.

I looked up at Dad, and he just smiled reassuringly and put his hand on my shoulder. "Let them be."

Dr. Underberg breathed in and out, then reached for her. "It's good to see your face. At last."

She broke into the first true smile I'd ever seen her wear. "Dad," she whispered. "It's good to see yours."

I smiled, too, and leaned against my father. We were home.

AUTHOR'S NOTE

Throughout the writing of the Omega City books, it was important to me that, whenever possible, Gillian and her friends deal with things that exist in the real world. Since these are books about truth and lies, I wanted to portray a world as close to the truth as I could make it. Though Omega City, Eureka Cove, and Infinity Base may be fictional, I wanted the technologies and experiments they found there to be things that used to exist, already exist, or theoretically exist and may be made reality in the near future.

Sometimes, I found, my writing moved slower than the pace of invention, and certain technologies (like self-driving cars) became commercially available sooner than I'd expected. Whoopee!

In space tech, we're a little behind the Shepherds when it comes to work on things like artificial gravity and health of our space travelers. Currently, the record for Americans in space is held by Astronaut Scott Kelly, with 340 days in 2015–2016 (slightly more than Dr. Underberg did, though Kelly is way healthier, I hope!). The world record is held by

Russian Cosmonaut Valery Polyakov, with 438 days, back in the 1990s.

I've read the reports on the amount of radiation they were exposed to, and the eye damage astronauts suffer in microgravity. Space is . . . not good for our delicate human bodies, I'm sorry to say. But I'm hopeful that if we keep working on these problems, space travel will become as probable as self-driving cars, because I still want to go . . . don't you?

Unfortunately, just like the tech is real, other aspects of this story are real as well. There are companies and organizations out there like Guidant and the Shepherds who are dedicated to lying to the public in order to make themselves rich and successful. I don't necessarily think any of them have a super cool space station hidden among the stars, but they can still hurt us with their deception. It's up to us—just like it was to Gillian, Eric, Savannah, Howard, and Nate—to ask questions, dig deeper, and discover the truth, no matter how complicated or difficult it might be.

Keep searching!

ACKNOWLEDGMENTS

A trilogy is an epic task, especially one that ranges as far as Omega City. I'm indebted as always, to my family, particularly my husband, who walked me through at least three or four versions of an ending to this tale. I'm so grateful to have made this journey with my editor, Kristin Rens, and the team at Balzer + Bray, as well as my extraordinary cover artist, Vivienne To, who really outdid herself this time around. Thank you so much to my writer friends for support: Carrie Ryan, Mari Mancusi, K. A. Linde, Erica Ridley, Heidi Tretheway, and most of all to Lavinia Kent, who actually let me hide out in her basement and fed me tacos for days while I revised this book again and again.

I'm also indebted to those who provided me with research materials, particularly the Space track at Dragon-Con, which is always an eye-opening experience (and where I first heard the term "hypothermic torpor"), and pretty much everything ever put online by NASA. Guys, your dedication to filming so much of your space exploration, from liftoff to landing, makes it so easy to describe what happens in microgravity. I also recommend Mary

Roach's excellent book, *Packing for Mars*, which was a gateway drug to so many dry NASA reports and so many delicious astronaut memoirs, and the podcast *99% Invisible*'s episode "Home on Lagrange," which introduced me to mad genius Gerard O'Neill and his book *The High Frontier*. If you want to read more about what a possible Infinity Base might look like, check that out.

I want to thank Eleanor for turning me on to the joy of hexaflexagons through Vi Hart's YouTube tutorials. I never realized the real Savannah Fairchild was hiding out right under my nose. You gave me the perfect puzzle to finish out my series.

And for all the readers who have come so far with me, thank you from the bottom of Omega City to Infinity . . . and beyond.